Vengeance
Follows

ALSO BY SCOTT LAX

The Year That Trembled

Vengeance Follows

A NOVEL

Scott Lax

With many Thanks and high hopes

Scott Lax

GRAY & COMPANY, PUBLISHERS

CLEVELAND

Library of Congress Cataloging-in-Publication Data
Lax, Scott.
Vengeance follows / Scott Lax.
pages cm
ISBN 978-1-938441-41-7
Wives—Crimes against—Fiction. 2. Revenge—Fiction. I.
Title.
PS3562.A9524V56 2013
813'.54—dc23
2013027892

Gray & Company, Publishers
www.grayco.com

Printed in the United States of America
I

Where vice is vengeance follows.

– Scottish Proverb

For Lydia and Finn

Vengeance Follows

Chapter One

SHE STOOD IN SLANTED sun that filtered through the flat's single window. It was dawn in the springtime. She was naked and wore no makeup. The sunlight played with her blond hair and she smiled a half smile, the other half hidden inside her.

"Let's go to the le parc Monceau, Sam." She looked out across the low buildings, out beyond the low gray sky. "It's filled with ruin."

Then softly: "But still things grow there."

Her hair was wet from her shower. She walked to him as he sat at his desk. He touched her arm. She took her other hand and stroked his tangle of black hair. He leaned in to her and smelled the soap on her skin.

"I can't find new words about wine," he said. "I'm so tired but can't sleep."

She took him by the shoulders and pulled him up from the chair. She shoved him down lightly on the bed and climbed on top of him.

"There will always be wine and there will always be words. There won't always be us in this moment."

Sam felt a chill but did not speak. He was thirty-five and she was twenty-seven and they were still young and the life that rolled out beyond the Paris rooftops had no end.

Pallid Parisian light filled the flat. A breeze came through the window. A page of his writing fluttered up and floated to the floor. He kissed her neck and tasted her lavender soap and licked the salt from her skin. They slid and kissed with salty mouths on wet skin.

Afterward they held each other and let the breeze dry them. He fell asleep for three hours. When he awoke she was dressed and reading his writing and drinking *café*.

"Now we'll go to le parc Monceau," she said. She put down the papers and smiled her inside-out smile as Sam nodded yes.

Chapter Two

LE PARC MONCEAU WAS filled with birds that dipped, soared, courted.

Sam and Sophie walked through the park, with its Roman temple, Dutch windmill, waterfalls, statues, the medieval ruins that Sophie loved, as well as an odd stone replica of an Egyptian pyramid.

"Do you believe in the power of pyramids, Sam? The shape—the triangle—I've read it has some kind of power. Do you think it does? You don't, I can tell."

"I believe you," he said and held her hand tighter. They kept walking and came upon the tree that is said to be the largest in Paris, an Oriental plane tree, nearly twenty-five feet in circumference.

Sophie put her ear to the tree. "What if this tree could talk to us?" she said. "What would it say?"

Sam was silent.

"Shh," Sophie said. "Okay. I think I can hear it."

"And what does this tree have to say to us?"

"It agrees to hold the memory of our love." She smiled, excited. "This tree holds our words. Oh, Sam, say something you want it to hold."

"Sophie. You know I'm not a New Age guy. I'm not the romantic you are."

"Really?" Sophie asked. "If that were true you'd write, 'This wine tastes good and that wine tastes bad and the other wine tastes medium.' I think you're a total romantic. You just need me to keep proving it to you."

"Sophie, look." Sam put his arms around the huge tree and closed his eyes. "I will love Sophie forever."

"That's much better," Sophie said.

They left the huge old tree that now held their memories and walked holding hands. The sun retreated shyly for the night as it does in Paris. The air and the earth and their skin cooled and it felt good to them, fresh, quiet. Sam and Sophie entered the café where they had met.

Chapter Three

SAM BECAME FRIENDS WITH a café owner named Virgile after he moved to Paris from Chicago. Virgile played music on his CD player that Sam liked, mostly American jazz, but also some French music by Françoise Hardy or Serge Gainsbourg. Sam thought the worst of it was corny but did not want to tell that to his only real friend in Paris, and anyway, he learned a little French by listening, though what he learned were mostly romantic expressions. When he tried them out Virgile laughed.

"Maybe some day you will have a woman to say these words to," Virgile had said.

When Sophie had first come to the café with her friends, Virgile insisted on introducing them. Sam knew he was in love right away. He thought he knew her, or remembered her, yet he neither knew nor remember her. He knew of no science or religion that could explain this instant connection, only that the reason had to reside somewhere outside of thought or belief, somewhere unseen and unknown, where perhaps all truth lives.

He believed something else: that Sophie was out of his reach, with her blond hair and blue eyes that looked right through him and the confident air that seemed to envelop her and protect her from the world.

One day, about three weeks after they had met, when he had drunk too much wine, he finally asked her out.

She'd smiled and asked, "What took you so long?"

Instead of going out they went to his small flat and made love. Sam felt satisfied and safe. Sophie felt this way, too, but it was only she who said it out loud. She soon moved into his small flat. After three months they married. She worked in sales for a local wine distributor and began to tutor Sam in the finer points of wine so he could make some money writing about it. He had had little luck with his short stories or his travel articles, which tended to dwell on obscure areas in the south of France—le Midi—that were of little or no interest to his editors.

Over time, Sophie taught Sam about wine and how to write about it, just as she taught him about love and how to show it.

"You let love breathe, like wine. You let love fill your senses, like wine. You let love help you to see beyond your pain, like wine," she would tell Sam. "And when you are not drinking wine you take that feeling and let it be a part of you. Remember the feeling and breathe your words into your writing."

She cautioned him to respect wine as one must respect love in its delicate balance. "What is the Scott Fitzgerald quote?" she said one evening as they walked the wet cobblestone streets. "'First you take a drink; then the drink takes a drink; then the drink takes you.' Is that it?"

Sam smiled. "Yes," he said.

Sophie looked at him.

"Good. Never let it overtake you. Just be you, Sam."

Chapter Four

Café virgile was about a half mile from the park. Sam thought of the tree they'd both touched earlier and in that moment he felt that they would live forever and nothing ever could hurt them.

They liked the café—everything about it, the atmosphere, the music, the wine, the food. Virgile cooked *cuisine bourgeois*, simple home cooking with curry and spices that was presented simply. Sophie ordered the *blanquettes*. They were always good but especially tonight because the air was cool and the sun had set. Sam ordered the *daube Niçoise* and a bottle of Château Sociando-Mallet red Bordeaux 1992. Virgile had good wines at prices they could afford and he, as did Sophie, taught Sam about French wine.

"Just bread for me, Virgile. I'll eat from Sam's plate," Sophie said in French. Her mother was French, an exchange student when she'd met her father in San Francisco. The language was as natural to her as English.

Sam and Sophie returned to their flat long after the sun had gone down and they had eaten and drunk enough wine and wanted nothing more than to be close to each other. Sophie

lit two white candles on her bedside table. She undressed and
put her clothes away on her shelf in the bedroom. Her clothes
smelled of her and of the sweetness of the park.

Sam sat on her side of the bed and they kissed. It was night-
time and in this poor part of Paris it seemed quieter than usual.
He walked the few steps to the bathroom to wash and brush his
teeth. He took his clothes off and put them on his shelf in the
bathroom. His clothes were heavier than hers. He walked back
into the bedroom. A full moon shone through the window and
lit Sophie's face.

Sam lay down beside her and put his hand on her back. His
hand rose and fell with her breath. He listened to Paris: voices,
car tires on cobblestone, music that rose up and faded and
repeated in patterns of rock, jazz, African, traditional French.

Sophie rolled over and faced Sam and ran her hands across
his arms and shoulders.

"Do you think the breeze feels nice, Sam? I think the breeze
feels so nice." She looked at the ceiling. "In Paris it always rains
this time of year, doesn't it? But I like the rain and the clouds
when they move over the Louvre and the rain drums the roof
of the terrace. Remember the day we waited out the rain? It
lasted forever."

"We never made it into the Louvre."

She looked at him under the light from the moon that
covered his face, then she slid toward him and they kissed. She
moved her body on top of his.

She kissed his neck and he kissed hers. He took her dark
blond hair and stroked it, then fluffed it so that it fell over her
face. He traced her skin from neck to tummy and ran his fingers
down her back on each side of her spine. She grabbed the back
of his hair with her hands and put him in her and began to move

back and forth and side to side and closed her eyes. East African music from the café downstairs grew louder as they moved in opposite circles.

She moved down and kissed his throat. He stopped moving and she pushed the top of her head into his chin. They pushed against each other, stopped, pushed again and moaned. He felt her sweat, tasted it. Her skin reminded him of the ocean. He saw her half-closed blue eyes, again the ocean, felt her hair that fell across his face. Afterward they lay in their pool of ocean-sweat; yet hers was sweeter, he knew.

"Are you glad we married?" Sam asked.

"Every day."

"Neither of our families were there," Sam said. "Only poor Virgile and the magistrate. And the drunk."

They laughed. They had never learned his name.

"I should have done better by you."

"I don't care about any of that, my dark Norwegian," she said. "What I care about is that we're together."

Sam took Sophie's face in his hands. The East African music in the restaurant on the street was playing just for them. He wanted to be nowhere but here, forever.

"I don't want anything to change," she said. "I love you," she whispered. "Do you know that? You must know that."

"I love you more," Sam said, as if they were teenagers. In that split second of clarity offered by the breeze and music and solitude and love, he wondered aloud how life might have been for them had they met earlier.

"That's not possible," Sophie said, her voice fading, her face softening with sleep.

*   *   *

When Sam woke up the sun was on the other side of the room and it was morning again. His life was here now, not in Chicago. He could never imagine going back to the States. He thought he had come to Paris to write, but in the thin morning light with Sophie by his side, he knew he had been somehow drawn here for her. Everything had brought him to this day, to this room, to Sophie. He heard Bach's "Komm, süsser Tod" from a radio in the flat next door.

It was Sunday. Sam decided not to try to write today. He loved Sophie and there was nothing that could come between them. They were still at the beginning of their lives together. The breeze came in through the window and covered them like soft cotton. Sam wrapped his arms around her, closed his eyes again. Soon their breathing was soft, even, and deep.

Chapter Five

SAM AND SOPHIE WERE happy with their simple lives made full and rich from being in love and in Paris. They hoped to have a child someday. There was plenty of time.

Then Sophie's headaches began. The first came on at a customer's wine shop. It was followed by others, their frequency increasing. She did not tell Sam because she knew he would worry. He had happily asked if she were pregnant when she vomited unexpectedly one morning in the bathroom. Unfortunately no, she'd replied. Something she ate the day before, she said. When they got very bad she was convinced she had developed migraines, so she went to see her doctor, an older man, a homeopathic doctor she trusted.

Sam and Sophie could see a sweet chestnut tree from their favorite table at Virgile's café. One early summer afternoon, the leaves were pale green yet bright, absorbing the cloudy light as the moon absorbs light from an unseen sun that requires no accolades or attention, a sun solitary and satisfied at being reflected.

The bark on the chestnut tree was easier to see under clouds. Sophie once told Sam that it was so alive it was as if blood was ready to burst forth out of it. She imagined the tree's roots wrapping around all of Paris from beneath the city. She said that she imagined the chestnut tree's bark was gray from holding every memory of every person who had ever noticed it, that its leaves were light and green because they chose to forget.

Sam was lost in writing about the wine that they both drank. Sophie could see in Sam's face that he was happy. She knew it was because she had given him a love he'd not expected, a love he didn't think he deserved, yet a love that fit him. She knew her love had made him whole for the first time in his life, before her eyes.

Sophie watched the shadows darkening the chestnut tree. She thought first of Sam, of what her impending death would do to him. She wondered if she should tell him what the doctor believed: that the kind of severe head trauma she'd survived in college was the reason for her tumor.

After her appointment, she had read everything she could about it: doctors had been studying it for decades, if not longer, but they couldn't agree whether head trauma could cause a brain tumor. Sophie's doctor was sure, however.

Now, tonight, Sophie decided that Sam needed to know what was wrong with her, and what her doctor had said.

Sam sat very still, and as he listened she saw him turn to a frozen rock. She talked of her happy childhood, then her days at college, her piano playing. She spoke of her friends, of the excitement of beginning life as an adult.

In quiet tones she told him of her rape in college and its aftermath—at least what she could remember. How she had wandered, dazed, from an off-campus apartment back to her dorm. Within days she had left school, never to return. She'd tried to recover in her parents' home for three months. She never reported the rape. Once it was over, she wanted it to stay over, to disappear.

She had told the Parisian doctor that she had recovered from that trauma, that the headaches had gone away for many years and that the memories of that night had faded. The Parisian doctor disagreed. He pointed to her head. "Your tumor began with trauma. You may seek a second opinion, a third. But . . ." He shook his head back and forth. "Your tumor began with trauma. This I know. This I know. *Je suis désolé, Sophie. Je suis désolé.*"

Sam begged to know the name of the man who had raped and beaten her. She in turn begged him to let it go, but she could see he would be tortured even more if he did not know the truth. They argued as two lovers who want only to continue loving. She gave in and told him.

Lee Clayborne, she said, had raped her, had beaten her head against the floor.

Where is he now? Sam demanded to know. Sophie told him that she had heard from a college friend that Clayborne was in a small town in the midwestern United States. That he was wealthy, successful, a pillar of his community.

Sam felt his heart blacken and felt a violence rise in him that was as a foreign body entering his soul.

"You cannot do anything about it now, Sam. I will be gone. You must go on, *you must promise me*: that you will live your life fully and let your hatred die along with me."

Sam did not answer her. Instead, with tears washing his face so that he could not see, he held her and they made love, one, twice, many times throughout the night. As if their lives depended upon it.

When they were finally spent, Sam said only, "I will love you forever. My love, my love. Sophie, my love."

Sophie finally slept, and Sam stayed awake. He believed the

French doctor. It was the only explanation. And he could not forget.

"I will love you forever," he said as Sophie slept.

It was there in the tiny, crummy flat she so loved, that Sophie lay down, on their bed, for once and all. Sam focused on her beautiful gray eyes that looked up at him when the pain abated for a few minutes. He watched her face grow grayer as her life drained away. He cried often. She was too weak to cry. The doctor came by to give her pain medications but knew there was no more to be done.

One evening, when the low Parisian sun turned the outside golden and the streets shimmering wet, Sam needed to say something to her. He waited for her to awaken from her nap.

Finally she opened her eyes.

"Sam?" Sophie said quietly, startling him. "Could you open the curtains?"

Sam got up and opened the curtains and looked back at her. Sophie had turned her head away from the window. Sam touched her lightly on her shoulder. He wept until he could barely see, his tears landing on her hair.

"Sophie? I will let it go, the hate I feel for that man. Like you wanted me to promise. I'll live my life. Sophie?"

Sam took Sophie by her shoulders and moved her gently so he could see her face. He instantly knew she had not heard him. She was gone. And so too was his promise to her.

Chapter Six

On a dull flat day in February, Sam dressed in jeans, a long-sleeved white shirt, his thick blue sweater from Norway, and boots from Denmark.

All Sam wanted of Sophie's was a photo, taken by Virgile, of Sophie and him at the café. It was Sam's favorite photo of her. She'd thought she was out of the frame, but she was right there in the eye of the camera, and it caught her thinking and unaware. Her face, the look in her eye, remained mysterious to Sam, even more so in death.

When he asked, she had said: "I was thinking of us being together forever. That's all."

After Virgile gave the photo to Sam, Sam wrote Yeats's lines on the back of the picture:

How many loved your moments of glad grace,
And loved your beauty with love false or true,
But one man loved the pilgrim soul in you,
And loved the sorrows of your changing face.

He wrapped the framed photo in newspaper. Then he packed a book on French wine, his notebook and pens, and his toilet articles, and put them in his suitcase.

Sam put the rest of his clothes, as well as all of Sophie's clothes, in her suitcase. He took their radio and left it outside the door of an elderly neighbor. He put everything else in the apartment in two green plastic garbage bags, walked down the stairs, and threw them in a trash bin behind the building.

He returned the key to his landlord and gave her cash for the four months left on his lease and said good-bye.

Carrying his suitcase and Sophie's, Sam took the Métro to the Armée du Salut.

At the Salvation Army there was a worker at the front desk, a woman in her sixties named Dorothée. Her face sagged from the weight of others' problems. She rose quickly when he came in and walked around the counter and stood in front of him, as if to catch him.

"*Êtes-vous d'accord?* Are you okay?" Dorothée asked him. She had seen thousands of stricken men, of every age and type.

Sam said, "I'm here to . . . to give . . . these clothes. They are mine and my wife's."

He put down Sophie's suitcase and remained standing holding his.

When Dorothée didn't answer, an exhausted Sam told her that his uncle had worked at the Salvation Army on the south side of Chicago, that the uncle was a good and kind man, but that Sam had not talked to him in years.

Then Sam began to cry, began to wobble, and collapsed into Dorothée's arms. She took him into one of the rooms for the homeless and lay him down.

The room was clean and painted blue. There was a cot, a sink, and a metal chair. A small desk had a lamp and a bud vase containing a single white tulip. A painting of Jesus Christ, done by one of the former inhabitants of the room, hung over the bed.

Sam, who had not slept in two days, immediately fell asleep. Dorothée checked on him every hour or so and brought him orange juice, biscuits, and ham when he would awaken and call out for Sophie.

The next morning he rose early and left, leaving a note:

Madame Dorothée,

I thank you for your kindness and for saving my life last night.

—Sam.

Sam walked to the nearest Métro and left Paris.

Chapter Seven

Ville de Rachat, France
Four Years Later

ON A SUNNY DAY in April, a yellow cat appeared on the path near the front door of Sam's cottage in Ville de Rachat. It looked to be no more than a few months old and was skinny but seemed healthy. Sam sat on a stone bench outside the front door and watched it skitter in and out of the wild lavender that grew in the untended flower beds. That afternoon, he put a bowl of cream outside his door.

Every day after that the cat visited Sam and drank the cream and ate the cheese he left out. A few times it left a mouse. When the cat wasn't looking, Sam took the mouse by its tail and tossed it into the woods that led to the stream behind the cottage.

Each day, when the cat came by and Sam saw it through the open door or window, he would walk outside to pet it. Shy at first, the cat slowly became accustomed to Sam. Then Sam would place the food on the worn stone pathway. Once the cat had finished eating, Sam would invite the cat to come with him. Always, the cat pondered Sam and trotted away until one day in mid-May when it followed him inside. Sam named the cat Truffaut.

*   *   *

The weather in Ville de Rachat was all things: warm, hot, cool, and cold. There were drenching rains and lots of sun. There were mistral winds and gentle breezes. Babies were born. Villagers died, usually from old age. There were many weddings and few divorces. Sam came to know the grocer, the butcher, green-grocer, the baker, and many farmers and wine growers. And in particular, his next-door neighbors, Erasmo and Micheline.

Every week or two, Sam accompanied Erasmo and Micheline, who were childless, to the local restaurant, where he was called *Le Veuf*—The Widower. For this he was respected and left alone when he desired, which was most of the time.

In the mornings, in his half-sleep, Sam watched the fan turning slowly above him. Sometimes Truffaut put a paw on Sam's face. Sam would lie motionless and think of his life with Sophie as if it still existed. Again and again, he relived their courtship and their marriage. His waking dreams would stop at that day at Virgile's café in Paris, on a late afternoon in early autumn, when the chestnut tree was still bright and green. He no longer recalled their walk back to the apartment, nor the hours after that, when she had told him about the tumor that was growing in her with such terrible speed.

After he arose in the cottage, Sam showered and shaved and made coffee. Sophie had liked him fresh and shaved, and they had always drunk coffee together in the mornings in Paris. His morning routine was the same here in the village until it came time to have coffee. Then he drank it alone.

In the afternoons Sam walked the hills behind his cottage or down to the sea in front of it. He walked by lavender fields and vineyards and olive groves.

He listened to the waves in the evenings. Hour upon hour

would go by with nothing in Sam's mind but the sound of the waves.

On cool evenings he put his hands in the deep pockets of the sweater that he'd bought in Norway, where he and Sophie had honeymooned.

There was a radio in the cottage, but he did not turn it on. He could not bring himself to listen to music. Every note reminded him of Sophie, who, in her soft, warm voice, had sometimes sung or talked him to sleep on restless nights.

He sensed his body at the cottage as he sensed the wind or the rain, connected to it yet separate. His sexual desire had disappeared after Sophie died. His heart darkened, his soul closed off, his body became lean and grew stronger in the sunshine and sea breeze and from the medieval pace of Ville de Rachat, a forgotten town, far from the glamor of the south of France.

He felt the rise and fall of the temperature through the seasons, the movement of the leaves and grasses, the dust from the paths that wound through the village and fields.

Virgile came to visit him after he'd left Paris. Upon seeing him, Sam's throat constricted and he couldn't breathe. He had to excuse himself and go for a walk outdoors. Virgile accepted his damaged friend as he was. A Parisian, he understood that beauty and decay could be simultaneous. Out of friendship, without Sam having to ask, he stopped visiting.

Now it was Erasmo and Micheline who stopped by at least twice a week to check on him. Micheline had been a banker in Paris and was now retired. Erasmo had made a small fortune brokering exotic cars. They, too, were respectful of his silent mourning.

Sam began to think that the breeze carried his and Sophie's past in the way she had believed the tree held on to their love.

When it moved through the trees, he remembered her life even more than his own.

At night memories would come to him as waves lashed the shore below the cottage, until, finally, after he'd drunk enough wine, as birds began to sing and light entered through the cracks in the shutters, Sam would pass out, his soul haunted by the woman he loved and the man who he knew had slowly killed her.

Sam had a peasant's health as he turned forty-three in Ville de Rachat. He ate local fruit and vegetables, the bread made at the bakery two kilometers from his cottage, the meats and cheeses produced from animals in and around the village.

On his one trip to the doctor, which he made at Erasmo's insistence, the doctor examined him, shrugged, and pronounced him fit and told him to keep doing whatever he was doing. Sam had recessive Sámi, Black Norwegian, genes so his skin turned brown in the Mediterranean sun. His black hair became streaked with white. After Sophie's death, the first streak had occurred almost overnight. Then the streaks increased until they mixed evenly with the black and he was nearly unrecognizable to himself.

Chapter Eight

SAM SAT OUTSIDE, HIS thick sweater keeping him warm. He scratched Truffaut behind his ears. The cat purred and looked at Sam with its green eyes.

Erasmo emerged from the path between their houses and put down a case of his brother's Buzet on the small stone terrace outside Sam's front door. Though the December day was clear and cold, he wiped the sweat off his balding head with a kerchief. He ignored the formality of *bonjour*.

"My brother never trusts the chemicals. He refuses to spray the vines in the seventies and eighties. All the other *vignerons* laugh at him. Now these same *vignerons* call their wines organic—simply because they do not spray poison. To Jean-Claude, wine is pure, was always pure. This is how God intend it."

Sam picked up a bottle and looked at it, turned it in his hand, put it up to the sun to try to gain a sense of its color.

Erasmo looked into Sam's eyes.

"Jean-Claude and I give this wine to you, Sam. We read your magazine articles, we read your book. Your writing is quite excellent in some ways. You understand *terroir*, and many things technical. Yet . . . you need to know *l'âme du vin*. The soul of wine."

Sam continued looking at the bottle.

"Perhaps the French translation was lacking," Sam said and smiled.

"*Vous comprenez?*" Erasmo said. "The soul of wine?" He took the bottle and tapped it. He laughed in a short, pleasant burst, then nodded. "Jean-Claude believe it have healing powers." He shrugged. "Maybe so. The vines go back to the days of the Romans. Similar to Bordeaux. Yet different."

Erasmo paused and studied the bottle. "Jean-Claude put his life into this bottle."

"Please tell Jean-Claude I am honored," Sam said.

"This is not to honor you." He took a corkscrew out of his pants pocket and without ceremony uncorked the Buzet. He sat the open bottle down on the stones that were cooling as clouds covered the sun and a wind came in from the sea. He stood up and walked into Sam's cottage to fetch two Bordeaux glasses from the set of six that he and Micheline had given him. He brought out no food, though it was ten in the morning.

Erasmo poured two glasses, filling each past its one-third-filled normal pour.

Sam put his nose in the glass and inhaled.

"*Mon Dieu*," Sam said. "*Divin.*"

"*Allez, buvez-le*!" Erasmo said. "Just drink! Don't talk."

Sam took a small sip, allowing some air to enter his mouth at the same time as the wine. He sucked it to the back of his mouth, swished it, closed his eyes, held it for a moment, and prepared to spit.

"*Non!* Do not spit this one."

Sam swallowed.

Erasmo took the glass from him and put it down. Then, ignoring the traditional tasting sequence of sipping, spitting, and repeating, he drank his own first sip as well, a more vigorous one than Sam's, as he chewed, slurped, and swallowed.

Sam opened his eyes. Erasmo handed the wine back to him. "Tell me."

Sam took another sip.

"I have never—"

"*Je sais.* I know. It is not like wine."

"Not like any wine I've tasted."

The two men drank in silence as clouds gathered over Ville de Rachat. They felt the salt from the sea on their faces. They finished the first glass, then another. Erasmo poured the last of the bottle into their glasses.

"It's a beautiful wine, Erasmo. Jean-Claude . . ."

"Jean-Claude know this, of course, Sam." Erasmo stroked his face. He ran his hand through his thinning hair.

"He make six hundred cases. In five years they help him retire."

"To do what?" Sam asked. "Such a great *vigneron*. And he's not old."

"Jean-Claude wish to go home to Normandy. To be with the rest of his family. To leave the grapes to another."

"I have a friend from—"

"Normandy. Of course: Virgile. I know. That's why we are all here. You in the cottage of the family of Virgile. Micheline and I in the cottage of my family. Our two families go back in friendship three hundred years. Maybe more."

Sam swirled the last bit of Jean-Claude's masterpiece in his glass.

Erasmo studied Sam's weary eyes and the lines that now marked his face. He looked at the streaks of white that had come to his black hair. Though his body appeared healthy, Erasmo sensed Sam was dying.

"Sam. Jean-Claude and I are brothers, but we are a different type of brothers. We don't need to talk so much. I speak for both of us. And for Micheline."

"All right," Sam said. He felt the warm wine running through him.

"Wine is many things, Sam. You have knowledge, yet you do not really understand it, any more than you understand yourself."

Sam remained quiet.

"May I go on, *mon ami?*"

"Please."

"Wine is not about being good or bad, about tasting this way or that way. Wine is about tragedy, the tears shed on the soil upon which it grows. About children born in the *châteaux* and love being made in the morning before the grapes are picked. The grapes hear all, see all, sense all. The rain and sun, the rot and ripening: these are functions of God. The rest, Sam, what makes wine of the spirit . . . this is of man. This wine we have shared: this is Jean-Claude's finest. He knows that. His heart is in this wine. When Jean-Claude taste it, he call me. I drive to his *maison* at dawn. I take one sip, Sam, and I know."

"I don't understand."

"But you do. You have drunk this wine."

"That it is the finest wine, the finest I'll ever drink," Sam said.

"*Non, non, non.* Not the taste, Sam."

Erasmo studied the clouds that were growing darker. The two men didn't speak for a couple of minutes.

"This wine is for your dying soul. For you to let go of Sophie and allow her to be at peace. For you to be at peace."

Erasmo stood up and took the wineglasses into the house and washed them and placed them on the shelf over the sink in Sam's kitchen. He walked back outside and stood over Sam.

Sam stood up and picked up the case of wine and held it out to Erasmo.

"Thank you, my friend," he said, giving the remaining eleven bottles back to Erasmo.

"These are yours, Sam," Erasmo said.

He took the case into Sam's cottage. A moment later he came back out. He took Sam by the shoulders. Erasmo had tears in his eyes. He clasped Sam's face in his hands.

"This wine is for you, Sam. To replace your poisoned blood so you can live. Wine can turn from sublime to vinegar in an instant," Erasmo said. "From good to bad."

He stared out at the sea.

"A man can turn from good to bad in a moment such as that," he said and snapped his fingers. "When you are ready, I hope that you will tell me what has happened to your soul."

"Why?" Sam said finally, looking at the sea, past the horizon.

"Because, Sam, you no longer have the look of a man who grieves for his dead love. *Tu as l'air d'un homme qui a de la haine dans son coeur.* You have the look of one with hatred in his heart."

Sam didn't reply. Erasmo tried to look where Sam was looking, but he could not. It was beyond his sight. Neither could he know that Sam no longer walked away from something. He was now walking toward someone.

Two days later, Sam Koppang left Ville de Rachat for America.

Chapter Nine

FROM THE TOP OF Grove Hill he looked out on a snow-covered village. It was nothing like the lavender village he'd just left behind in France. Neither did it resemble his native Chicago, where Lake Michigan was to the east and prairie flattened out from the skyline to the west. Here he could see an entire village in an ancient glaciated valley, a village where Indian tribes once fished and hunted in and near the banks of the river that ran through the town, and then later, where settlers from Connecticut hacked out the Western Reserve. A worn stone wall that was built by the Works Projects Administration in 1940 sloped down from across the street to the bottom of Grove Hill. Powdery snow bent the branches on evergreen trees. The last of the sun slowly faded, the sky now light pink as in Paris but so much colder.

Days earlier, he'd resumed smoking for the first time in twelve years. The heat and cigarette smoke from the opened door of his rented car drifted into the still, icy night and hung in the air. He left the car door open, his suitcase on the front seat. He was in no rush to go inside the clapboard house. As he stood still in the cold, his body began to relax from the hours of cramped flying and driving.

The Realtor had told him the door would be unlocked and the key would be on the hall table.

"You're coming to Chestnut Falls," she'd said on the phone and let out a light laugh. "Nobody locks their doors."

A police car drove up East Summit Street and stopped. The driver had a gray crew cut. Fifty-eight-year-old eyelids drooped over weary eyes. He drew down his window.

"Everything okay?"

"Moving in," Sam said, walking toward the cop, his hands casual but in full view, a smart move that hadn't changed in centuries of encountering armed authority. He nodded toward the house, then back toward the village.

"Pretty town."

"They're—we're—proud of the Christmas lights. The Jaycees put them up. Good bunch of guys, if a little on the frat-boy side. They like their beer. One or two punks, but you get that anywhere, I suppose."

"Jaycees?"

"Junior Chamber of Commerce."

"Oh, right. It's been a while."

Sergeant Michael Shield, retired New York City street crimes detective, could tell. The new guy was no local.

He paused, looked down Grove Hill, then looked at Sam again. He could be Black Irish with his wavy hair and his Anglo features. Or Jewish. You couldn't always tell. Maybe he shouldn't have said "Christmas lights."

"Holiday lights," the cop said. "I never get tired of looking at them. People complain when they go up too soon in the fall, but I wouldn't mind if they were on all year. Life's tough enough. Light helps."

"Little white lights. They have them up all year in Paris."

A motorcyclist drove through the center of town, revving his engine, jarring the quiet night air. He turned left on West Orange Street and headed out of town, toward Cleveland.

"That's a Harley," the cop said. "Sounds like a Baker Six-Speed. That's what I drive. Drove."

"I never rode a bike. Never had the guts," Sam said.

"Wiped out three times, nearly killed myself twice. That's not guts. That's crazy."

"Crazy's understandable in a crazy world," Sam said.

"I don't ride anymore. That where you moving from? Paris?"

Sam's and the cop's eyes were parallel highways into town.

Sam glanced at the cop. "By way of a small town in France."

"You mind me asking? You don't have to answer. Personal question. Not police business."

"Ask away."

"Your business here?"

Sam leaned down and looked into the cop's eyes.

"I'm a magazine writer."

Sam had crushed out his cigarette on the driveway. He stood up, kept his eyes on the cop.

"I know it's not exactly popular these days, but do you mind if I light up? Rough couple of days. Lots of travel."

"I'm not a fan of Big Brother saying what we can and can't do to ourselves," the cop said, nodding at the cigarettes. "Those'll kill you. But so will a lot of things."

The cop took a cigar from his ashtray, stepped out of the cruiser, and lit it. He stood about six feet, same as Sam.

"I can't even smoke in the cruiser anymore," he said. He took a couple of puffs. "You smoke these?"

"I have a box of Cubans packed in the car. My next-door neighbor in France gave them to me as a going-away present.

You'll have to come over and have one with me sometime. Arrest me afterwards."

"'As if,' like my daughter would say," the cop said. "I'm not going to cuff you because of a couple of stogies. That's Customs, anyway."

The cop blew out smoke. He waited. Finally Sam said:

"I write about wine. I write about wine and the places where they make it—Europe—France, Italy, Spain, Germany, you name it. California, Latin America, New Zealand, Australia. I went to South Africa once."

He hadn't traveled for years—since before Sophie died, but Sam skipped that.

"That right?" the cop said.

"Sometimes I write stories about people in the wine world."

"Which people?"

"People my editors think will sell their magazines. People who make wine. I like them, for the most part. In fact I can't think of a *vigneron* I don't like."

Sam paused, took a drag. "The wine—"

"Winemakers," the cop said and laughed. "I get you. Go on."

"But also people with too much money or too much time. People who probably shouldn't be written about."

Sam looked away and listened to the quiet of the town.

"Your high-society types," Sam said. He dropped his cigarette on the ground and crushed it out with his foot. The cop looked down.

"But it pays the bills, right? Nice boots"

"Made in Denmark," Sam said.

"They make wine in Denmark?" the cop asked.

"Got these in Germany. Reingau. Pretty place. Like here. They make some good wines."

"We have some writers here," the cop said. "There's a children's book writer down the street. And a guy who wrote for the movies lives just east of here in Bainbridge. He wrote that movie for Sharon Stone and Michael Douglas. The ice pick movie? You see that?"

"Ice pick? Not that I recall," Sam said.

Sergeant Shield did the math. The stranger had been away for a long time.

"There was a funny papers writer, but he moved away. He liked his privacy."

"This seems private," Sam said.

"It's not. Small doesn't mean private. You want privacy, go to New York. Lots of people hiding in plain sight."

"I don't know much about other writers," Sam said. "We tend to avoid each other."

He lit another cigarette. They stared down Grove Hill into the glittering village.

"I'll quit. I never should have started up again."

"Free country. I told you, it's none of my business," the cop said. "Something made you start up again. It happens."

"'Writers seldom wish other writers well.' Saul Bellow said that. He was a good writer," Sam said.

"I heard of him. I read, too."

"I didn't mean . . ." Sam said.

"This is a good place to write, I bet," the cop said.

"Maybe," Sam said. "We'll see. I don't know how I'll react to putting down roots. I'm giving it a year or so."

Shield got back in his cruiser. He wouldn't get any more out of the other man tonight. Sam stuck his hand in the window and shook the cop's hand.

"Sam Koppang."

"I'm Michael Shield. I've heard all the jokes so don't bother."

"Good to meet you, Sergeant," Sam said, glancing at the stripes on Shield's jacket.

"Writers and cops," Shield said, tapping his left sleeve stripes with his right hand. "We both notice things without letting people know. Both try to figure out how people's minds work. Both use information others miss. That why you guys like to write about us guys?"

"Don't know. I don't write about cops."

"Both know silence is golden," Shield said, drumming on his steering wheel.

"True enough."

They two men looked toward the village. Shield said, "Got to make my rounds. Welcome to Chestnut Falls."

He put the cruiser in gear. "You'll get sick of seeing me. I'm not forgetting that Cuban cigar offer, by the way. Congrats on getting them through customs." He winked at Sam.

"Hope I'll see you around," Sam said. "I don't know anybody else here."

Both men knew Sam had made a mistake. Neither man flinched.

"People call Chestnut Falls 'The Bubble,'" Shield said out his open window. "It's hard to do anything here without everyone knowing about it." He smiled.

"The air can get rancid in a bubble, though," Sam said.

"If you only knew," the sergeant said. "I got a thousand stories. They'd make a good book."

"I don't doubt it. You should write it."

"You hear that a lot, huh? Everybody thinks they got a story."

Sam looked at the lights. "Sure, I hear it. But the thing is, Sergeant, everyone does have a story."

"But not everyone can write it. That's what makes you different."

Sam looked at Shield's face, a road map of creases. Sam wondered where all those roads had taken him.

"You take care, Sergeant. Keep the streets safe," Sam said.

Sergeant Michael Shield turned left on Grove Hill and drove down into the village. Sam watched his taillights blend in with the town. He lit another cigarette, exhaled, and studied the view. He saw a lighted church spire just east of the main street that ran through the village, and what looked to him like a Greek Revival building of some kind on the west side of the street. He had a clear view of a park at the center of town. He made out a bandstand straight out of the nineteenth century, and brick walkways, plantings, and benches. He squinted and thought he saw an old-fashioned telephone booth at the top of the park, which formed a triangle, the vertex facing uphill where he stood. He wondered if the phone booth worked, if anyone used phone booths in America anymore, or if it was merely a novelty. He saw a tall pine tree covered in multicolored lights at the southeast corner of the triangle. He saw shoppers walking in and out of stores and the bars and restaurants at the bottom of the hill. He heard faint music on a PA system. Nat Cole sang "The Christmas Song."

Sam's stomach tightened. He could not bear to hear the song, but he listened anyway. He'd loved to sing to Sophie when she was alive. Now it was time to listen to what he had not been able to hear and observe what he had not been able to see. Here he had the time and space to confront her past, to try to understand the horrors he believed had caused her death.

"I miss you, Sophie. Every day," he said aloud.

His words were a cloud of smoke and frost. He threw his cigarette down and stamped it out. He took his suitcase from the car and walked toward the front door of the rental house.

The house was cool when he entered. He turned the thermostat from fifty-five to sixty-five and heard and felt the furnace kick in. He felt a trickle of heat come out of the floor registers and smelled the dirt and soot from the old filter. He took off his sweater and hung it in the hall closet.

Lee Clayborne didn't know Sam existed, much less that the widower of the woman he'd raped and beaten in college now lived in the same quiet village. If Sam were to come to terms with her death, he would have to look Clayborne in the face. Somehow, when he saw his eyes he would know what to do next. Maybe then he could find some peace in his shattered heart.

Chapter Ten

THE YOUNG WOMAN WITH cropped auburn hair called to him from his bed. "What's taking you so long?"

Lee Clayborne didn't answer. She—Heather? Holly?—hadn't earned his answer. She wasn't worth an answer.

This red-haired bitch could lie there and wait. He liked to make them beg for it. Charm, seduce, then wait until he heard the breath heavy from excitement or nervousness. Leave them in the dark for a while.

From his bathroom, he heard her giggle from his bed.

"You're a strange one," she called out. "I thought you wanted to . . ."

"Minute," he said, his voice high and bright and youthful, as he moved to the doorway to look at her lean, pale body, half covered in his bed, only candles casting light on her. He smiled the smile that had closed dozens of land deals as well as these deals. Deals were deals. Property was property.

He closed the bathroom door. She said something he couldn't hear.

"Shut up," he whispered.

He looked in the bathroom mirror. Days before Christmas and he was still tanned from Thanksgiving in Turks and Caicos.

Lee ran the fingers of his left hand up his right arm and up to his neck. He wondered, as he had so many times before, why he could not find a woman with skin as soft as his own.

He poured out a tablespoon of cod liver oil, brought it to his mouth, swallowed, replaced the cap, rinsed the bottle off, and dried it with one paper towel from a roll under the sink. He put the roll back it its place. Then he put the bottle in his medicine cabinet next to his other supplements. A machine that works perfectly needs only preventative maintenance. He didn't need some fat doctor to tell him that in ten years.

He brushed his teeth and rinsed with mouthwash and walked slowly back into the room.

The slender, red-haired woman sat up and uncovered her breasts.

"I thought you'd left me," she said. "We were just getting to know each other. Come here." She stretched out her arms to him.

Lee took her face in his hands and kissed her gently. He moved his hand down to her crotch. He stroked her. Gentle. Considerate.

"You're ready," he said.

"Yes," she said.

He smelled the Champagne on her breath. He sniffed so she could hear him sniff. He lowered his voice—the lightness and brightness disappeared.

"You're drunk."

His voice hardened.

"No penetration. I don't want you calling me up in two weeks telling me you're pregnant. I don't . . ."

He paused, closed his eyes. *Bitches*, he thought. *They all want too much from me.*

"I do not want to hear *that* from *you*."

"Hear what? What the hell are you talking about?" she said, her voice shaking. "What's going on?" She drew back, pulled the five-hundred-thread-count Egyptian cotton sheet over her breasts. Her eyes grew wide in the dim light.

"What?" Lee said, his voice a whisper as he grew hard. "What?"

"I'm just asking what's going on," the woman said.

"What?" Lee said, more excited now. He grabbed the back of her hair and pulled her head toward him.

"What do you *think* is going on? Do what you came here for," he said, putting his hard penis in her mouth, one hand still pulling her hair, the other pushing it down. "Don't even think of biting down." He laughed. "Or I'll break your fucking neck."

Four minutes later, Lee Clayborne turned the lights on. He was naked, still hard. She could not speak, which didn't seem to surprise him. She watched Lee pick up her clothes from the floor and hand them to her. She shook so badly she wondered if she would be able to put them on. As she fumbled with her clothes, her heart beating so strongly she could hear it in her ears, she saw Lee's bedroom: polished walnut floor; ebony table with a blue crystal vase and fresh flowers; a dresser with a framed photograph of a dog, though she had seen no evidence of a dog; a Pop Art painting, with blue and black shapes that writhed on a white background, on the white wall opposite his bed; shut mahogany closet doors. The matching mahogany door to the bathroom he had emerged from a few minutes ago was closed.

She couldn't look at him, but sensed he was watching her dress. He smiled at her and said, "I'll call you."

His tone was calm and, she thought in a growing panic, friendly. She began to tremble all over and could not speak. She dressed quickly and forgot her small purse, which was on the floor by his bed. Lee picked it up.

"Here," he said. "Take your purse. No excuses to come back. I wouldn't like that."

She was still unable to speak. Her neck began to ache.

Minutes later she was in her car headed home toward Garfield Heights. It did not occur to her that he didn't seem to want to call her again. She only remembered she'd given him her number earlier in the night and suddenly she felt sick, as though she might vomit in the car. She held it in, sheer will. She flipped open her phone and called her cell phone service provider and changed her number without considering the number of friends and family and business associates she'd have to inconvenience. She could still hear her heart beating in her ears. She wondered whether she was having a heart attack.

Worried that her breath smelled of booze and him, nearly frozen by the sight of her smudged mascara in the rearview mirror, she drove home carefully so as not to be stopped by the police.

The red-haired woman glanced down at the McDonald's wrappers on the floor of the passenger side of her black Corolla. All she cared about was getting out of Chestnut Falls and back her apartment that she never wanted to leave again.

Chapter Eleven

THE MAGAZINE WRITER ON Summit Street had a face Shield couldn't read and a story that didn't make sense.

Koppang smoked, but then a lot of them smoked in Europe. Koppang was alone, but lots of guys that age were alone. He figured the guy was what—thirty-five, forty, forty-five? The age they divorce. There were lots of them alone in this town, going to the same bars, fishing in the same waters. They drank too much and screwed the wrong women and fell asleep in their cars after the bars closed, or almost ran down some poor sap walking home, trying to avoid his own drunk driving. There were messed up guys in look-at-me cars everywhere.

Yet Koppang didn't seem like one of those men. Michael Shield had too much experience to go after the usual suspects when everything pointed toward the usual suspects. When evidence pointed toward the usual suspects in New York, he'd looked elsewhere.

When the muscle had been Chinese and a Chinese bar owner got his teeth knocked out when he wouldn't pay the bagman, Shield talked to the Russians or Irish. When he called in for backup on a used weapons raid in Harlem and the backup didn't come, he didn't blame dispatch. When three slugs hit just above and below his knee and another opened his femoral artery, he didn't blame the cops who were trying to drive through a rainstorm to get to him as he nearly bled to death.

When Michael Shield hit the ground and opened fire and emptied his 9mm and killed his snitch Danny Wu because Danny Wu's old Iver Johnson Saturday-night special had jammed when he tried to fire a fifth time at Shield, he didn't blame Danny Wu for setting him up because that was Danny's job.

Michael Shield had learned, over nineteen years on Street Crimes in New York, that sometimes it's not who or what you think it is. It's often somebody else.

That applied to civilians and their problems. He guessed that applied to Koppang.

What bothered Sergeant Michael Shield of the Chestnut Falls Police Department was that he liked Sam Koppang and that meant he was worried about him.

Whatever Sam Koppang was in trouble about, or was running from, Michael Shield had no idea. But why was he here? Koppang didn't seem like a player. Maybe he'd gotten involved with the wrong people somewhere.

Yet Michael Shield sensed there was something else going on, something that could mean trouble not just for Sam, but for others. Sometimes, he knew all too well, from decades of experience, that people in trouble end up looking for more of it. And they'd usually find it.

Chapter Twelve

SAM SLEPT FOR TWELVE hours and awoke just before noon. The furnace wasn't putting out much heat, and he could see his breath in the cold air. He wondered if he should check the filter. It had been a long time since he'd lived anywhere with a furnace.

There was a cast-iron woodstove in the kitchen. The Realtor had mentioned it. He hadn't given it much thought at the time, but now he was glad to have it. It was a different cold here from the Mediterranean coast, where the mistral winds had blown through the cracks in his cottage door walls and sent him to bed, under the blankets, with a bottle of wine on his bedside table. There, the winds died down eventually and the sun came out.

The front yard at the Summit Street house was small and tidy. The backyard was a hill that merged with the backyard of a house on Cottage Street to the south. His yard was covered with piles of dried brush and discarded branches from pruned trees.

He pulled on a pair of jeans, a long-sleeved T-shirt, a sweater, wool socks, and boots.

The back deck of his house rested on stilts. He walked out onto it and saw a heap of logs that looked like it had been there for several winters. It was evident the house's most recent owners hadn't used the woodstove.

Behind the logs Sam found a roughed-up wicker basket with a handle. He walked down the wooden deck stairs and began collecting small branches and twigs for kindling.

"You're new."

Sam looked down the hill at the rear deck of a house on Cottage Street. A woman with shoulder-length salt-and-pepper hair stood smiling at him.

"And you're on my property."

Sam heard classical music coming from inside her house.

"Sorry. I didn't know," Sam said. He returned her smile.

The woman wore brown corduroy pants, mud- and salt-stained Wellies, a mustard-colored chamois shirt, and gloves. Her cheeks glowed bright pink against the cold

"There's a property marker buried in that brush pile there."

She looked at a large pile of old branches and leaves to Sam's left.

"I'm too lazy to dig for it. But it's absolutely no problem," she said, looking away from him while gathering up a few dry, well-cut pieces of firewood. "You can take all this brush and then some. Don't just stand there staring. Come down the hill and introduce yourself."

Sam traversed the hill sideways. "Sorry," he said, nearing her back deck. "I just arrived last night. Thanks for not shooting me."

The Bach was difficult for Sam to listen to. Sophie had loved Bach.

"Ha," she said. "My dad did teach me to shoot a squirrel at a hundred yards."

"I've never even held a gun," Sam said.

The snow fell again. Sam was getting colder but he liked the feeling.

"I'm Sam."

He put out his hand. She took his hand and looked him in the eye.

"I'm Ellen. And I'm freezing."

She turned, picked up another log from the neat stack on the back of the deck, and opened the sliding door to a blazing fireplace.

"Come in and have a shot of Christmas whiskey."

Sam put down the wicker basket and walked into Ellen's country kitchen. The walls were painted in rusts and golds and the cabinets were walnut. Pots and pans hung from ceiling racks. China lined the shelves. There were three stockings hanging from the fireplace embroidered with "Ellen," "Adva," and "Ringo."

Ellen took a tumbler from the wet bar near the fireplace.

"Neat or rocks? I'd heard someone had moved in."

"Neat. Please."

"Of course. I heard you're a writer. From somewhere in Europe . . . France? Or so the local fuzz tells me. You're allowed ice cubes here," she said and smiled.

Ellen turned on the wet-bar tap and whisked the glass under it.

"A little water will open it up," she said, handing it to him. "Just a few drops."

"How did you know I drink?" Sam asked, looking at her bookcase filled with books on art, film, and psychology.

"You're a writer, right? So you either drink or were a drunk. And now I know you drink. I'll give you the benefit of the doubt and assume you're not a drunk."

"Not as a rule."

He held up a book on Alexander Archipenko.

"Are you a writer, too?"

"I sculpt. You picked out my favorite, my hero. Archipenko. Negative use of space," she said. "Makes for good art. Makes for a pretty good life. It took me a long time to learn that."

He heard keys working in the side door. A woman came in

with a brown-and-black mutt on a leash. The woman's skin was deep olive. Her blue-black hair was covered with melting snowflakes.

"Hello," she said to Sam. She didn't put her hand out.

"Sam, this is Adva," Ellen said. "And this is Ringo."

Ellen bent down and held Ringo's big head in her hands and gently shook his head back and forth while he tried to lick her face. "He's my favorite little Beatle, aren't you, boy?"

Adva looked at Sam. Ellen gave Adva a quick kiss.

Sam thought he saw Adva blush.

"You're okay with this, right, Sam?" Ellen said.

"I just moved here from France," Sam said. "I hope that answers your question. If not, yes, I'm okay with that."

"Well, that's good. That makes two of us. Her"—Ellen looked at Adva—"I'm not so sure about."

"I'm sorry?" Sam said.

"Just a joke," Ellen said. "I hope."

"I'm not sure I understand," Sam said. "You two are together, right?"

Adva drew back, looked at Ellen, and raised an eyebrow at Ellen.

"I'm sorry about that, Sam. Some residual insecurity I have. And I'm sorry, honey," she said to Adva. "And yes, we're together."

Adva took off her long shearling coat and hung it on a coat tree. She walked to the stainless-steel pot on the stainless-steel gas range and stirred the contents. Sam smelled the curry. Then Adva went to the wet bar and poured herself some vodka. She opened up a bottle of tonic and topped it off and put a slice of lime in it.

Sam looked at the fire. Ellen sat on a leather love seat by the fireplace and Adva joined her, snuggling into her shoulder.

"Sit, Sam," Adva said.

"I should go. I don't want to interrupt your afternoon . . ."

"Look, I'm a shrink. I'm usually good at first impressions. It's kind of a curse. So something tells me you don't have much else to do. It's Christmastime. Sit."

Adva got up and refilled Sam's glass.

"The stew will be ready in a half hour. Why don't you join us. I hope you like vegetables."

Sam sat down on the Amish-made rocking chair across from them. He closed his eyes and listened to Bach. He heard logs crackling and Ringo's nails tapping on the wood floor as he walked out of the country kitchen and into the living room. The dog trotted up the stairs: enough visitors for the day.

The two women allowed a long silence.

"I'm not sure what day it is," Sam said finally.

"Sunday," the women said together.

"Ah," he said and opened his eyes. He wondered if they could see the tears that had crept into them for the first time in years. Both women had kind faces. He was too tired to care if they could see, so he looked into the fire.

"How did you two meet?"

"Lots of time for that," Adva said. "You're the new guy. Tell us about you. Were you always a writer? High school poetry prodigy?"

"The opposite. I was a bit of a jock. Or tried to be."

"Baseball, right? You look like a baseball player," Adva said.

"Football. Special teams and defensive back. Second-string. The pride of Curie Metropolitan High School," he said and laughed. "But I did start two games when a guy got hurt."

Ellen rose and took three bowls from the rack over the sink. Without looking up she said, "Okay. So we know you were a football player . . . more or less. Here's the deal, Sam. You tell us more about you. If we like what we hear, you spend Christmas with us. If we don't, you spend Christmas with us."

Sam looked outside and felt the warmth of the room. His thoughts were jumbled from the whiskey he'd drunk too quickly. He knew he had to leave.

"Yes. I'd like that."

Back outside, Sam's mind flashed on the room at the *Armée du Salut*, where he'd spent the night when he collapsed before he left Paris forever and moved to Ville de Rachat. There were good people there, and in Paris, in this small town, and back home in Chicago. Why had he come here? To see the face of the man he blamed for Sophie's death? What if the doctor had been wrong?

Chapter Thirteen

AFTER REHAB FOR HIS leg, after sessions with the department's PTSD counselor, Michael Shield decided to retire early from the New York City Police Department. He was ready to leave the city. Margie had skills she could use anywhere—numbers don't lie and people with money always need bookkeepers. His pension allowed him some flexibility. It was time to slow down. He answered an ad in a law enforcement trade publication for an opening in a small town department in Ohio. A geographic cure.

Margie, simply happy that her Mikey was still alive after being shot and left for dead, was willing to live anywhere with him. Anywhere safe. She packed up his Meritorious Conduct medal and family photos to take in their own car and had the rest of their belongings put in a moving van. Unlike Mikey, a lifelong New Yorker, Margie didn't look in the rearview mirror as they crossed the George Washington Bridge.

In Chestnut Falls they used the eighty-five thousand they'd made from selling the old place to pay half the purchase price of a nice little house with an attached garage. It had a yard where Mikey could grill steaks and Margie could plant tomatoes. It had a basement for Mikey's model trains. It was perfect.

*   *   *

As part of Michael Shield's new job with the Chestnut Falls Police Department, Chief Steve Getzer had asked him to sit in on the Village Council meetings. He needed someone to turn on the tape machine to record the minutes and lock up the Town Hall when the meeting was over. Not much overtime in it; the council meetings were one night a month.

Now, fourteen years later, Sergeant Michael Shield coasted through this routine. Turn on a tape recorder, daydream about model trains or the Yankees or whatever for two hours, lock up, go home to Margie.

The only thing that bothered him about the job was the current council president. The blond good looks and bashful smile that had helped him get elected to four two-year terms left Shield more than unmoved—they gave him an uneasy feeling he tried to escape when he'd left the City.

The charitable work the council president did for the arts, for the homeless, for you name it, meant nothing to Shield. He wasn't impressed by his being a "green" developer, either. Whatever he called himself, as far as Shield was concerned, he still chopped down old trees and built gigantic houses on eroding hillsides.

Michael Shield believed, from the moment he met the man, and after he'd heard how that man had treated his ex-wife, just as he believed tonight, at the last Council meeting of the year, two nights before Christmas, that Chestnut Falls Village Council president Lee Clayborne was a world-class prick.

Chapter Fourteen

BY 6:00 P.M. ON Christmas Eve, one block down Grove Hill from Sam Koppang's rented house, Whirly's Main Street Grill was emptying out.

Whirly's had survived every trend since it opened in 1948. A shot and beer joint from its opening until the early seventies, it then had a brief incarnation as a biker bar until too many drug deals and too much betting action got it closed in 1975.

Six months later it reopened, but proprietor Ernie Whirly had lost his heart for slinging burgers, pouring beers, taking bets, and making small talk. One summer's day during a heat wave, Ernie locked his bar for the last time.

After Ernie Whirly took his oxygen tank and fishing rod and retired to North Carolina, local investors bought it. The former Whirly's reopened as a fern and Chablis bar called the Main Lodge. Ten years later, after ferns and Chablis went the way of parachute pants, it closed up and sat vacant for nearly a half decade.

In 1989, the first African American proprietor in the village of Chestnut Falls in forty years reopened it as Whirly's Main Street Grill. Johnny Kenston, a Vietnam vet who had cashed out of his carpet-cleaning business, returned the bar to its small-town roots.

Johnny used the old name for the Whirly Burger but added fresh herbs, used better cuts of meat, and made the best burgers in town, which he served with french fries that he hand-cut and seasoned himself. Johnny also established a large beer list, from cheap domestics to imports to specialty craft beers from New York and Wisconsin.

He taught himself about wine and specialized in Californian and Italian. He got to know the local distributors. By the mid-nineties, Johnny had a well-rounded wine list and a reputation as a straight shooter who ran an excellent bar.

He began serving homemade pizzas, gyros, and soups, and attracted a loyal clientele that ran from old-money multimillionaires with patches in their khakis to landscapers and bricklayers with mud on their boots. Whirly's was a local favorite for girls' nights out; women knew Johnny didn't allow bad behavior from men.

Most townspeople liked Johnny. They knew he'd had a tough time as a result of Vietnam and respected how he'd rebuilt his life and achieved modest prosperity. Johnny, in turn, knew Chestnut Falls as well as anyone. He saw it with an outsider's eyes. He'd grown up at The Camp, the all-black enclave a mile south of the village. That he had few black customers now didn't surprise him. With a history that included both the Underground Railroad and the Ku Klux Klan, Chestnut Falls had elements of entrenched racism its residents seldom acknowledged.

Johnny acknowledged it, if only to himself. In his sixty years, he'd learned how to read people. In this very white town he could tell who the bigots were by how overly friendly they were to him or if they looked at him for too long or too short a time.

When the Wednesday afternoon all-male lunch bunch came in, Johnny knew which of the retirees were sick and which were hurting. He knew who had lost a wife and how many grandchildren each one had. He knew who had power and who affected it—rarely the same thing.

He knew when a patron was about to lose it over a cheating spouse or dying loved one. "Time to go home," Johnny would whisper kindly. "You don't need any more trouble. We'll be here tomorrow."

He'd never had a wife—he'd been serious twice, engaged once, but it had never quite worked out. Now he was alone and needed to take care of himself. His path to retirement was clear. If it took working twelve hours on Christmas Eve, so be it. As much as he liked his work, it was getting to be time to move on.

At six-twenty, Lee Clayborne and his friends Ethan and Tom entered the bar.

"Gentlemen," Johnny said, as Lee and his friends walked in, "Happy holidays."

Lee stared at the young woman behind the bar, grabbed Johnny's hand in both of his and shook hard.

"And a very Merry Christmas to you, my brother," Lee said. He looked around. "Let us drink to the spirit of the holiday," he said, his voice now louder.

The bar was slowly clearing out as patrons headed home for Christmas Eve. "You're a beauty," Lee's friend, Ethan, said to the bartender as the three sat at the bar. "And working on Christmas Eve, no less. You new? Got a name?"

"Working Christmas break," she said, wiping the bar in front of the three men. She glanced at Johnny. "After that I hope to stay on."

"Name?" Ethan said, drawing out the word. "Do you have a name?"

After a three-second pause she said, "Rachel."

"Your major? Don't tell me. Let me guess . . . Psych? Sociology?"

Lee Clayborne leaned forward. "Leave the guessing to the

pro," Lee said, slurring the word "guessing" and staring at Rachel. Both his friends remained quiet.

Johnny walked over and stood behind the three friends.

"What'll you gentlemen have?" Rachel said. Johnny watched.

"Let me ask you something," Lee said, looking at her breasts. "Pretty girl like you. Working on Christmas Eve. You're what . . . twenty-one?"

He pulled his gaze up to her eyes and smiled.

Lee turned to his friends.

"I'm good at this. Watch."

"I'm twenty-one, yes," Rachel said. She forced a smile as her left eyelid began to twitch. Looking at Ethan, she said, "And I'm an early childhood education major."

"Where," Tom demanded.

"What'll you have?" Rachel said, trying and failing to force a smile.

"I said: Where do you go to college?" Tom said.

"Kent State. I commute," she said, regretting it immediately, knowing she'd said too much already.

Rachel cleared her throat, braced on the bar with both hands, voice quavering just a little. "Do you gentlemen want a drink?"

"Wait," Lee said. "I'm getting this. Likes little kids. Lives with Mommy and Daddy? Am I right?"

Rachel didn't reply. Her eyelid twitched again.

"Favorite color? Pink. Likes kitties. I'm going to keep going. You're working on Christmas Eve. You're Jewish."

Rachel inhaled quickly and looked at Johnny. Johnny moved forward and put his hand on Lee's back.

"Tell you boys what. I'll buy you a Merry Christmas drink and then we're closing up. Sound good?"

Lee moved his shoulder so that Johnny's hand slid off. He lowered his head and sneered up at Johnny.

"We *boys* want your bartender to join us. You've got nothing to do tonight, do you, darling?" Lee said. "I mean . . . you know. You're not exactly going home to sing 'Silent Night,' are you?"

He lowered his voice. "So join us. I have a present for you."

He leaned toward Rachel and whispered loudly, "I like exotic women. My ex was exotic. She was brown. I mean, *swarthy*. How about it, *Rachel?*"

It was the first time her name had sounded obscene to her.

The oxygen was momentarily sucked out of the room. All the other patrons within earshot were speechless.

"I'm no bigot. I'd do you," Lee said.

Lee reached for Rachel's arm. She drew back. Johnny grabbed Lee by the back of his coat and pulled him up. Lee began to resist, pulled his hand back to hit Johnny, but before Johnny could take him down, Ethan and Tom bum-rushed their friend out the door.

Lee flailed and screamed at Johnny: "Fuck you, you piece of shit!"

Tom, the biggest among them, locked Lee in a bear hug and wrestled him into the passenger side of Lee's BMW SUV. Ethan poked his head back in the door, as if he'd simply broken up a shoving match on the basketball court.

"Johnny . . . hey . . . sorry, bro. Lee had a bad day." He shrugged and smiled. "He's putting up a housing development. The bank called his loan and the damn thing's tanking. He's hammered, man. You know how it is. We're taking him home . . ."

"Take him home," Johnny said, his voice strong and steady. "But you're all out until Saint Patrick's Day. You guys hear me?" he said, poking his head out of the door. "Don't come back until after March seventeenth. Merry Christmas."

Johnny slammed the door. He turned around and faced the

room. Two young couples sat in front of the gas fireplace. Three middle-aged men were putting on their coats on the other side of the bar.

"Last call. On the house, folks," Johnny called out. He forced a smile, ignored the burning pain in his gut. After all these years . . . "Then go home and hang your stockings."

"Are you all right, Rachel?" He turned to face her. "Listen. Lee Clayborne. He's not to come in here again. I mean *never*. You call me if he comes in and I'm not here. I'll tell Albie, too, and the other bartenders. I told his buddies that they were all okay to come back after Saint Paddy's but not him. He's out permanent. I don't like him. I'll take care of it if the time comes."

Temporary banishment from bars was public punishment for bad behavior in Chestnut Falls. Permanent exile was a public slap, a humiliation that got around and marked a person. Exile meant you had disrespected the people behind the bar or you'd started a fight, which could mean jail. This was not the sixties or seventies—Whirly's was no longer a punch palace. Johnny intended to keep things that way.

Johnny Kenston had been to Vietnam and done things that he hadn't talked about in decades. He had recovered, as best he could. Usually when small-town trash like Clayborne acted out, it bothered him for about twenty seconds. Tonight was different. Johnny felt threatened, and he didn't like it—especially not after all these years, all he'd endured.

"You just forget that boy, Rachel," Johnny said. "He's nothing. You go and have a nice holiday with your family. I'll close up."

Johnny lightly touched Rachel's elbow and led her out from behind the bar. He helped her with her coat and opened the door.

"I'll see you on the twenty-sixth," he said. "The college kids will be out in force. I'll need you."

They hugged.

"Thank you, Johnny," she said. "Merry Christmas."

"Happy holidays, Rachel."

Johnny watched her as she walked out into the snowfall, brushed the new snow off her VW Bug, and drove away.

That night Rachel dreamed about Lee Clayborne. The next day, a day by family tradition when she usually joined parents and brother for Chinese food and a movie, she called her mother and told her she was sick. On December 25, Rachel Rosen stayed in bed.

Chapter Fifteen

SAM LOOKED OUT THE back window and saw that the Christmas snow looked too beautiful to ruin with his footprints. For the first time since he'd arrived, he left his house through his front door. He turned to the left for a few steps, walked down the salted sidewalk on the east side of Grove Hill for a half block, then turned left down Cottage Street. Adva and Ellen lived in the second house on the left.

Adva opened the heavy, white early-nineteenth-century front door.

"Merry Christmas." She kissed Sam on both cheeks. "You've brought something wonderful?"

Sam entered and brushed the snow off his blue sweater.

"No coat?" Adva said.

"Not yet," Sam said. "But this weather is bone chilling. Reminds me very much of Chicago."

Sam stamped the snow from his feet. "Merry Christmas to you, Adva. It's kind of you two to have me over."

He noticed a framed wall calendar, hung just inside the door, opened to March 1995, featuring a photograph of their historic home.

"Home Sweet Home" was written in red, in expert calligraphy, on the bottom of the photo.

Adva saw Sam looking at it.

"The only way anyone will get Ellen out of this place is feet first"

She shoved a hot cider and rum punch into Sam's hand.

"You will drink it and you will like it," she said. "Come and sit by the fire. No falling asleep."

She turned and led him through the living room and into the country kitchen, with a crackling fire. Ellen stood basting a turkey.

"I like the fireplace in the kitchen," Sam said.

"It's nice," Adva said. "This entire room was added years ago, which is why this place can't get an 'Historic Homes' designation. It bugs Ellen. And me, I suppose. Then again, the downstairs would be tiny without it."

Sam took the three bottles of the Domaine Brusset out of a canvas bag.

"I didn't know what we were having so I brought these," he said, waving his hand over bottles of white, rosé, and red wine.

Ellen glanced over at the bottles.

"That's good of you, Sam. Three bottles, though. Are you trying to get us drunk?"

Adva, who had thrown a few logs on the fireplace, walked over and picked up the red.

"Thank you, Sam. Very expensive looking. Was 2000 a good year for this?"

"A great year," he said. "French, made from old vines. Very balanced. I just wrote about it."

He hesitated for a moment.

"Sorry—if I bore you, please tell me. I can talk too much about wine. Sometimes I fake it. We all do."

"That I don't believe. And we could use a little variety around here," Adva said. "We're stuck on California wines. But they do what I need them to do."

"They do pack a punch," Sam said. "Well, that's not nice of me to say. California wineries do make some wonderful wines. I just don't much like them. Often too much alcohol, too much sugar, too much sun, too much irrigation, too much everything for my taste. Still, they often beat the French at wine tastings. So maybe I'll just shut up and stop insulting good wine and my hosts."

"Well, thank you for these. We'll try something new. And we'll like it," Adva said.

"I'm already trying something new—making a turkey dinner," Ellen said. "It's a pain in the ass."

Adva took Sam by his arm and led him toward the fireplace.

"Don't mind her. Christmas and my birthday are her main contributions to a year's worth of cooking around here."

"I'd be better at *shooting* a turkey," Ellen called out.

"Ellen kills innocent creatures," Adva said.

"My dad was a hunter, and he taught me. It's what you do in Wisconsin. And we ate what we shot. It's an Indian thing," Ellen said.

"She's the other kind of Indian. Native American, at least in part," Adva said.

Sam sat in the chair by the fireplace. Adva refilled his cider.

"I'm sorry," Sam said, as Adva topped it off. "Drank too quickly. Not used to parties."

Adva shook her head at him and raised one eyebrow.

"Loosen up. You're making me nervous."

"I'm a quarter Chippewa," Ellen said. "I'm simply saying I honor what I kill. You kill it, you eat it. Use the pelt if possible."

Adva turned back toward Sam.

"She hasn't hunted in the entire time I've known her. It's a myth, as far as I know."

Sam looked at Ellen, then back at Adva.

"You're a happy couple."

"Is that a question or a statement?" Adva said.

"A question, I suppose."

"Happy enough," Adva said.

"Dammit!" Ellen shouted. "Flipping marshmallows are melting too fast on the sweet potatoes."

She took the sweet potato casserole out of the oven.

"I try to make one fun dish and it's a crusty mess."

"You like burned marshmallows, don't you, Sam?" Adva said.

"I want to hear what you two are talking about," Ellen said. "Wait until I serve supper, okay? A half hour. Tell him about your work, Adva. I'm sure Sam will be as depressed as I get hearing about your head cases."

"That's inappropriate," Adva said.

Sam looked into the flames.

"Someone built a fine fire."

"Ellen. More Wisconsin outdoors skills."

"How'd you end up here?" Sam asked. He looked at Ellen, gave her small smile.

"Romance," she said, chopping a carrot, slower than an experienced cook, but carefully, the sculptor. "I was in love with a woman I met in college. She was from here. We settled in down in Madison, then she wanted to move home. Homesick for her parents, she said. I think it was someone else. But whatever . . . I followed her. Eventually we split up. She went back to Madison, and I stayed here. Funny, huh?"

Sam and Adva were silent. The fire popped and crackled, just short of roaring. Ellen checked the turkey as it roasted.

"I grew attached to this little town. Then I found this place and fell in love with it. I use the old stables next to it for my studio."

Sam looked out the side window.

"I thought they were garages," he said.

"Carriage houses, originally," Ellen said. "By the way, this house is cracked, if you didn't notice. Outside." She nodded her head over her right shoulder, toward the front door.

"The house had been moved, I don't know, sometime in the mid-twentieth century. Is that right, honey?" She looked at Adva.

"That sounds right," Adva said, then shrugged to Sam as Ellen went back to work, now stirring a pot of gravy. "Anyway, it didn't settle properly, has this big crack down the middle of the top, the portico, whatever you call it. So I got a deal on it."

"That's wonderful," Sam said.

"It is. It really is, Sam. Thank you. Like a gift my dad gave to me. This house and a place to start over."

"And?" Sam looked at Adva. Ellen stopped stirring and looked at Adva, too.

"And here is where I met the love of my life."

Sam smiled broadly now. "How did you two meet? Do you mind me asking?"

Adva shifted on the couch, suddenly uncomfortable.

"I was married," she said. "Let's not spoil the evening." She tried to smile, gave up. Now Sam and Ellen were quiet.

"I'm a therapist. I should have better words for the way he was. But he was, let's say . . ."

"A pig," Ellen said loudly. "A real piece of work. Abusive in every way: physical, emotional, financial. The trifecta of shitty behavior." Her temper had begun to rise but she calmed herself down. "And you're right, honey," she said, letting the food simmer as she walked to Adva, who seemed too vulnerable now to deal with the memory. "Let's leave it at that," Ellen said. She kissed Adva, and went back to the kitchen counter and stove.

Outside the snow fell in wet clusters. Ellen went back to slicing vegetables for the salad.

"Can I help?" Sam said, staying seated.

Ellen shook her head.

"She's on a mission," Adva said. "The cooking. There's some coming to terms with family traditions going on. We all have our crosses to bear." She shook the ice cubes in her drained drink. "She's forty-nine, Sam. And I'm thirty-five. And you are . . . ?"

"Forty-three last summer."

Adva pondered this for a long moment. "How old is she, if I might ask?"

"She?"

"I assume a she. Your former. Your ex. Whomever. I'm not seeing a he with you."

"I had a wife who died."

Sam had not eaten all day and had quickly drunk three strong rum punches. Suddenly it seemed there were no barriers.

Ellen stopped tossing the salad and put down her teak fork and spoon. They had a CD of vintage 1950s songs playing. Sinatra sang "The Christmas Waltz." Ellen walked to the CD player that sat atop an old, green, distressed table near the sliding-glass door to the back deck, and shut it off. Neither woman said a word. Ellen sat next to Adva on the leather love seat.

The sweet potatoes with the browned marshmallows cooled on the stainless steel countertop. The turkey continued cooking, its juice evaporating. Ellen's and Adva's eyes filled with tears. Sam's eyes remained dry.

Chapter Sixteen

AMANDA SHIELD, ONLY CHILD of Mike and Margie Shield, had never seen her mother so happy. It was one o'clock in the afternoon on Christmas Day and her father was in the basement with his new steam locomotive. Amanda knew that her mom had saved and splurged on it, bought it new, and now Daddy not only wanted to run it but felt obliged to because Mommy had been so excited to see him open it this morning.

"Daddy seems really happy this year," Amanda said to her mother. "I haven't seen him this way at Christmas in a while."

She put a tray of sugar cookies in the oven.

"He is. He's thrilled that you're doing so well. And he likes his job, Mandy. I think New York is finally behind him. He's slowed down."

Margie hugged her daughter.

"Maybe these are the beginning of our golden years," she said.

At dinner Daddy led grace. The three of them held hands

"Tell us about your acting, sweetie," Margie said.

"I was in an experimental piece right before break," she said.

"Please tell me there was no nudity," Margie said with a smile.

"No, Mommy. There was hardly any dialogue, either," Amanda said. "A boy in our class wrote it. It might have been the most boring one-act in history. It took place in a Laundromat and mostly we pretended to fold laundry while a couple argued about whether he'd been cheating on her. I had one line."

Amanda turned her expression to a grimace.

"'You should appreciate the fact that she even puts up with your stinking socks.' That was my line. I don't think I'll get nominated for a Tony Award."

All three of them burst out laughing.

Down in the basement, after dinner, Amanda said, "Aren't you missing your football, Daddy?"

"First year I haven't cared about it," her father said. "I don't need it. You and your mother are all I need."

The trains finally stopped for the night, and father and daughter climbed the carpeted steps of the finished basement. Mommy was asleep in the big rose-colored chair. Daddy and Amanda went to the kitchen.

"Beer, Daddy?" she said.

"Sure, sweetie. You get one too."

Amanda opened the two bottles of Budweiser with the Coca-Cola bottle opener fastened beneath the sink and gave one to her father.

"Merry Christmas, Daddy," she said.

"To you too, Mandy," he said.

"I wish I could protect you from that world out there," he said.

"You always have. You always will."

"If anything happened to you, that would be the end of your mother and me."

"Daddy, so morose on Christmas," she said. "You should have faith."

Michael Shield looked at his daughter.

"Of course, honey. I'm sorry. This is always an emotional day for me. And soon . . ."

"Soon?"

"You'll be on your own."

Later on Christmas night Michael Shield helped his drowsy wife up the stairs and into bed and climbed into bed after her. As he lay there, he thought about how the dangerous the world was and how Amanda had no idea what was really out there.

Sergeant Michael Shield had only shot and killed one person, which was one more than he'd hoped to kill. But as he fell asleep, he realized there was a silver lining to that horror. If anyone ever tried to harm his daughter, he knew he could, and would, take care of it.

Chapter Seventeen

SAM AWOKE THE DAY after Christmas and didn't know where he was. Then he heard cars slushing and whining up Grove Hill. He saw the winter sun glittering in through his window. He felt the slow ache of Sophie's absence. He remembered he'd spent the evening with Ellen and Adva.

Sam sat up in bed and saw the present they'd given him laying across the armchair in the corner of the room, a pair of black leather gloves.

He'd brought them only wine, which didn't count as a Christmas present.

"We have everything we need," Adva had said, when Sam thanked them and told them of his embarrassment over the gift. "Too much, in fact, so you're not allowed to get us any makeup presents. Just keep bringing wine."

It was a simple room, painted off-white, with its old furniture, supplied as part of the renter's deal. There was no slowly turning fan, no sound of waves. Truffaut was not lying next to him, purring, placing a yellow paw on Sam's face and looking at him, as if this alone would eventually prompt Sam to get out of bed and prepare the cat's milk and cheese plate.

From a south-facing window near his bed on the second floor, Sam had a clear view of the village.

Over the treetops Sam saw the forty-foot-tall blue spruce put up by the Jaycees. All the Christmas lights in town were on.

There was a park in the center of town. Instead of a town square, the park was in the shape of a triangle. Main Street, at its north end, toward Sam's house, separated into South Main Street and South Franklin Street. Sam could see the bandstand wrapped in a big red bow from his bedroom window. Lights and people and cars—everywhere Sam looked life exploded.

Sam threw off the sheet and the thick layer of old wool blankets he'd found in the closet. He wrapped himself in one of them and walked to the kitchen to boil a kettle of tap water for a stray teabag he found in a cabinet.

While the water heated, Sam took some logs and started a fire in the woodstove. He'd turned the thermostat back down to fifty-five, since the furnace was so weak, anyway. Ellen and Adva had given him leftovers from Christmas dinner. He took a cold plate of oyster stuffing and sat by the woodstove and drank tea and ate the stuffing and a small slice of the turkey that was drier than Ellen had hoped but tasted delicious to Sam.

Sitting in the stove's heat, with a blanket over his shoulder, he thought of the two women and how they had been kind to him and about this peaceful village in the midwestern United States, a place that neither needed him nor had hurt him.

He thought of how Sophie had given him all of her love and that because of her he finally understood sacrifice and loyalty. Why had he come here? To come face to face with a man he blamed for her death? What would he even say to him? That an eccentric French doctor traced her tumor to a rape and beating Sam couldn't even prove? Sam had no proof. He had no witness. He had nothing except what he sensed was true.

*   *   *

Sam showered and dressed. Perhaps if he drove around long enough, he would find someplace to spend the day—a bookstore or a wooded area where he could walk.

The sky was bright blue and the snow hung from the tree branches and reflected the sunlight. He drove through the village and turned left on East Washington Street. He drove for three miles until the street became a road and five more miles until the road became U.S. Route 422. He continued east. He drove until he passed the Pennsylvania border and then another few hours up into the foothills of the Allegheny Mountains.

Eventually, Sam pulled off the highway and went into a small, run-down but clean store decorated with Pittsburgh Steelers paraphernalia. The man behind the counter looked him in the eye. The man was bald and wore a Steelers jersey. Sam bought a coffee and a pack of cigarettes. He asked for matches.

"Where you coming from?"

"A little place east of Cleveland."

"Browns country, huh?"

The man smiled pleasantly and coughed a loose smoker's cough.

"Name's Chet," he said. "You a native over there?"

"No. I'm originally from Chicago."

"Heading to New York?"

"I'm Sam. No, just driving."

They shook hands.

"That right? Salesman?"

"I'm a writer."

"Okay. I like to read. I could read all the time. My wife likes the TV. You married?"

"No, not married."

"What you write about?"

"Well . . ." Sam looked around. "I write about wine."

"Wine? Well, that's something to write about, I guess. You can see our selection here. Nothing fancy."

"It's fine," Sam said. He walked down the center aisle and looked at the wine bottles for a few moments. "Tell you what. I'll take this," Sam said, walking over and plucking up a bottle of Columbia Crest Merlot. "Nothing wrong with this. This is a good wine, Chet."

Chet smiled, rang it up. Sam paid again with cash.

"Stop in again. You can tell me about the fancy wine world sometime," he said. "Like to learn new things."

"I'll be back. I enjoyed the drive."

"I'll be here. Go Bears. Doan' tell anyone I said that."

"Go Steelers," Sam said. He had missed American football.

Sam waved to Chet and left the store. He turned the car around and headed back west toward Chestnut Falls. He saw the road, obeyed the signs, drove the speed limit, all of which lulled him. After twenty miles he was not in Pennsylvania or Ohio, or America. He was in Paris, at le parc Monceau. He saw Sophie, even as he flew past the bare trees and low winter clouds, the median strips of dormant grass. Sophie, so beautiful the first day they went there together.

He remembered their conversation, the gentle admonishments she'd given him after he'd informed her he was an introvert, someone who abhorred violence and conflict.

"I don't buy it," Sophie had said. "You're tough, Sam. You're the toughest guy I've ever met, in fact. Mr. Viking. You think you're just a sensitive artist, but you're a tough son of a gun. Aren't you? You are."

Only birdsong and breeze answered. Sam was silent.

"Aren't you?" She'd held his hand tighter, used her thumb to stroke his hand, comforting him.

"I don't know why you say that."

"Well, you are," she'd said. "You could be alone forever and survive. Do you remember what you called your apartment when we first went there? One of your only French phrases, which you said with a little too much pride, as far as I was concerned."

"What did I call it?"

He asked the question though he knew the answer.

"*Ma maison de la solitude.* You called it your house of solitude, Sam."

"*Ma maison de la solitude,*" Sam said aloud in the car. "But you changed that, Sophie. You changed everything for me. I didn't ever want to be without you. I can't be."

Hours later, he pulled into his driveway, the low sun having traversed the sky as it dipped toward setting. Not until he shut off the car in the darkening evening did he realize he had not turned on the radio, for even a moment, during his drive.

Unless it was forced on him, he still could not bear to listen to music. Nothing, Sam thought, had changed. He realized that for the past hour, after his memory of their talk that day, he'd thought of nothing but of what could have happened on Sophie's lost night so long ago.

Chapter Eighteen

LEE CLAYBORNE ENJOYED THE preparation rituals for his annual day-after-Christmas party. This year, with business going downhill and Johnny Kenston publicly humiliating him on Christmas Eve, he was especially ready to party.

"I want to see new talent this year," Lee had instructed his friends. "Go to the malls, get some shopgirls, whoever's hot but I haven't met. I'm sick of the same chicks."

A Lee Clayborne party invitation was coveted within the aging hipster set in Cleveland. In a city with few actual celebrities, where chefs and local TV weathercasters took the place of actors and rappers, Lee Clayborne, by virtue of the charity benefit circle, qualified. He had appeared frequently enough in Cleveland's society pages to stand out from most of the typical party crowd.

The DJ avoided the hip-hop that Lee despised. Lee liked the old stuff: Al Green, George Michael, vintage Michael Jackson. The girls joked about the music when sober, but at Lee's private parties they danced to it until long after midnight. A few danced topless after doing shots. Lee could usually get a couple of the wildest to make out with each other in front of him.

At noon Lee began to ready his home in the historic district of Chestnut Falls, otherwise known as the Golden Ghetto. Lee hated the ironic misnomer and all it implied. On the other hand,

The Camp—the black section of town—now that was a ghetto, no matter how many of its older houses had been rehabbed. That was Johnny Kenston's part of town. And Johnny Kenston would never be welcome in Lee's universe. Johnny should never have thrown him out. He wouldn't have if he hadn't been too stupid to know what a truly good guy Lee really was.

Which wasn't an easy thing to be, especially after what his miserable father had put him through. His alcoholic old man never got over being what he called "a fallen WASP." If Lee had heard that term once, he'd heard it a thousand times.

"You'll never know what it feels like to be a fallen WASP," Lee's father would shout at his wife. "My goddamned ancestor signed the Constitution."

Lee's mother, a fragile woman so quiet that Lee had no memory of her ever raising her voice much above a whisper, would shrink into a corner of the kitchen.

"I'm sorry, honey," she'd say, though it was obvious she rarely knew for what.

"You're what?" Lee's father would scream.

"I'm sorry. You're right: I don't know what it's like."

"So you're calling me a failure? I work my ass off all day to feed these spoiled kids and you're calling me a failure?"

His father hit. Usually his mother, sometimes Lee, less often his older sister or little brother—but that wasn't the bad part. What his father did when he was very drunk was the bad part.

The bad part would happen so quietly that Lee thought he dreamed it until he was a teenager. Late at night. Basement. Darkness. Warm liquid in his mouth. Attention, stroking, soft words. Apologies. Tears.

Then, his father's voice, full of the sorrow of an irredeemably ruined man: "Back to bed. It won't happen again."

He'd hated his father and what he'd done to him. He'd waited for what seemed forever for his chance for his own redemption, when he'd no longer have to question his manhood.

In his senior year of high school, the time finally arrived. Prom.

A May night in Ohio. Perfect weather. The beer in a cooler in the trunk of his black Mustang. No Firebird or Charger for him—he was a Ford man, unlike his father, who still drove old-man Buicks.

His date didn't disappoint when he went to pick her up. Dana looked beautiful, her prom dress pink and satiny and showing her shoulders. There was a solid rock band. They played Lee's favorite song, "Eye of the Tiger," at his request.

Afterward there was a drinking party and sleepover out in South Russell. Lee and Dana sneaked into one of the rooms in the ranch house near the barn, which the host's parents had vacated. It was tradition. Lee had the foresight to realize, even at eighteen, that Prom would only happen once. He had brought condoms. Dana was ready. They'd discussed it in the corners of hallways at school, and in the car, and on the phone. When the time came to make love—the first time for both of them—they weren't too drunk.

When Lee tried to enter Dana, he was suddenly in the basement with his father.

Just close your eyes. He heard his father's voice in his head, over and over.

Lee couldn't stop sweating. He felt himself shrink as his penis crushed softly against her moist crotch, like a balloon with the air let out of it. Permanently soft, he thought for a moment. Would it never harden again? He felt sick, hopeless. Had his father turned him into a queer?

Dana, confused, laughed, tried to soothe him as she lost her own desire. "It looks like it's hiding from me." She giggled. "It's cute."

Lee rolled over. He couldn't get the old man out of his head, wished he could beat him to a bloody pulp, smash his head against the floor of the basement, let him lie bleeding, then kick him in his disgusting mouth.

He lay there for a few minutes and then rolled over on top of her, grabbed her hands and pinned her arms back.

"What are you doing?"

"Something different. Let's pretend," Lee said.

"Why are you holding my arms down?" Dana said.

"We're going to do something different," Lee said again.

"Different than what? I don't want to do this anymore."

"I do," Lee said, spitting on his hand and forcing himself inside of her.

"You're hurting me," Dana said. She started to cry. "I'm not ready, Lee. Ow, ow, oh my God Lee you're hurting me. Please don't do this."

Sobbing, she tried to move him off of her, but his weight was too much.

"This is what you've been wanting for the last two hours," Lee whispered harshly. "It's your fault it happened in the first place."

Dana bled and cried. Lee thrust hard until it was over. He felt at peace.

Dana cried for a few more minutes. When Lee finally rolled off of her, she asked him in a small, terrified voice to take her home. He said he was too drunk, and then fell asleep. When he woke up, Dana was gone, taken home by friends.

The next day Lee knew he had found a way out of the memory of his father in the basement and the path back to himself. The panic that had set in that night never returned: his father *hadn't* turned him gay. He was attracted to women, and he'd never doubt it again.

Before and after his marriage, sometimes during it, when the mood struck him, he'd find a girl or woman on the spur of the moment. He didn't discriminate against color or ethnicity. With his tousled, blond good looks, his angular jaw, his blue eyes, his ripped body, his many credit cards, finding sex partners wasn't difficult. After Dana, he usually kept the violence in his mind during sex.

In the parlor of Lee's large, well-kept house on Lincoln Street was an antique table from India. Sitting on the table was a zinc-top Coudanne & Cie birdcage.

Lee saved polishing the table for next to last when getting ready for his parties. He used a wood polish from Germany. It took about a half hour. The last thing he did before he shaved, showered, and made the first batch of drinks was clean the birdcage, which took close to an hour. He cleaned every wire in the cage with a special extra-thin cloth, polishing the zinc top. Then he cleaned under the birdcage, where no one could possibly see.

It didn't take long to clean the inside of the cage; no birds inhabited it. He had let those two loud, obnoxious, shitting, peach-faced lovebirds go one day after he'd gotten the table and birdcage in the divorce.

He'd insisted on the birds and birdcage and table in the divorce, but only after he and his ex had agreed to all the terms, waiting until she was ready to sign.

Adva's divorce lawyer was outraged and had called Lee's demand for the birds and birdcage punitive and cruel.

Lee disagreed. Adva divorcing him was far more punitive than a birdcage worth five grand. The table had been her grandmother's and he knew it was important to her. But Adva was taking away the only family that mattered to him—her. He was hurt and he wanted to hurt back.

The birds became nearly as hysterical as Adva when he put them in his SUV and drove off. He drove east into a rural area and drove around for an hour and a half until he saw two hawks circling. Then he pulled over, opened the Coudanne, and gave the lovebirds their freedom.

Tonight, as the party was about to start, his birdcage was impressive. When the first female guest arrived, a woman in her late twenties, she stared at the birdcage.

"Why don't you have a bird in there?" she asked.

"My ex got them in the divorce," Lee replied, smiled, and handed her a drink.

Chapter Nineteen

OVER COFFEE ON SATURDAY afternoon at Adva and Ellen's, Sam was asked to accept their invitation for dinner and a New Year's Eve celebration in downtown Cleveland.

Adva was friends with the chef at Lola on East Fourth Street and had managed to get a reservation. They had booked a room at the Ritz-Carlton, so Sam would need to take a taxi back to Chestnut Falls.

"We'll even pay your cab fare," Adva said. "We'll buy you dinner, get you drunk, kiss at midnight, and send you on your way."

"Please come," Ellen said. "If I hear one more of Adva's stories about cutter girls and emo boys who want to be gay, I'll go crazy."

"I never use names," Adva said.

"They all sound like one giant, wriggling mass of teenage angst. That's an era I can't get far enough behind me," Ellen said.

"Or we can talk about your installations in the living rooms of Hunting Valley," Adva said. "And your rich clients who keep us living in decadence." She raised her mug and an eyebrow. "This coffee, Sam? Fourteen dollars a pound. Can you believe that? Ellen won't drink Starbucks, much less Maxwell House."

"At least I don't take quarterly trips to buy my clothes on Oak Street in Chicago," Ellen said, and smiled.

"One of us has to be girly," Adva said.

"You know what?" Ellen said. "If you don't want to be with me . . . with me the way I am . . ." She stood up and walked upstairs, her footsteps lighter than her big-boned frame would indicate.

"I'm sorry, Sam." Adva said. "That was my fault."

Sam looked toward the fire, avoiding Adva's eyes.

"These things happen. People in love hurt one another, Adva. I even miss that."

"Tell me about the little village you were living in, Sam."

Sam talked a little of Ville de Rachat, of Erasmo and Micheline, even of Truffaut.

A few minutes later they heard the light footsteps returning. Ellen walked into the room her eyes bloodshot, her face in a tight smile. She sat down next to Adva, who took her hand, stroked it, and said, "I'm truly sorry. I was trying to be funny. But I wasn't funny. It was a stupid remark."

"Listen, Adva. Ellen. I really appreciate the New Year's offer. But I can't go with you two on Monday night."

"Why, Sam? You can't possibly be busy," Ellen said, leaning forward.

"I haven't celebrated the New Year since Sophie died. I just like to go to bed early and have the night over with."

"We don't like thinking of you sitting in that empty house of yours," Adva said. "Will you at least go down to Whirly's at midnight? Johnny gives out Champagne. Slip in and out and no one will notice the difference."

"You know what?" Sam said, relieved at the warmth returning to Adva and Ellen and happy to change the subject. "You two should get engaged, marry, and make honest women of each other."

"We can't marry here," Adva said. "This is Ohio. It borders Indiana and West Virginia, for goodness sake."

"And Pennsylvania," Ellen added.

"Go to another state. There are states where gay marriage is legal, right?"

Ellen slid her head down on Adva's shoulder.

"I'm not completely convinced of her orientation," Ellen said. "As you unfortunately just witnessed." She looked at Adva. "I mean, honey . . . you were married to a man."

Adva breathed in sharply. "It's not about orientation. It's about who you love," Adva said.

"Well. Love is love, isn't it?" Sam said. "I guess I'm saying I know it when I see it. And I see it here."

Sam stood up, said his good-byes, and kissed each of them on both cheeks. He left through the back sliding door and tramped up the hill to his house, where the fire he'd made that morning had died out. The house was cold again.

He rebuilt the fire and sat in front of it until his face was warm and he felt sleepy. In his half-sleep, he thought of Erasmo and Micheline in Ville de Rachat. He thought of his mother and father in Chicago. Both retired factory workers, both proud of their son, even if they didn't understand why anyone would want to read about wine, much less write about it, much less live anywhere other than the South Side of Chicago.

He'd written them once a month during his entire time in Paris. He had visited his folks in Chicago every other year, and had flown them to Paris on the alternate years. They'd adored Sophie and she felt the same.

They were good people and he felt lucky to have them as parents. Sam had sent them gifts from Paris every Christmas— an Hermès scarf for his mother, a case of Grand Marnier for his father.

Yet the Koppangs were stolid Scandinavians at their core. He never mentioned his little brother Anton, who had died in a bicycle accident when Sam was ten and Anton was seven. Neither did his parents bring it up to him. Grief was to be silently endured.

Sam loved them, but he hadn't felt like an American in a long time. That they were proud of him was the only way he could repay them for the happiest childhood they had been able to give him.

When Sophie died, he couldn't bring himself to tell them. After a few months, he wrote letters that contained lies of omission, as if nothing had happened.

The letters had worked, allowing him to report only good news, with the exception of innocuous, sometimes fictional problems that kept his mother interested.

The crazy old lady in the flat next door plays Edith Piaf day and night at full volume, he once wrote, prompting a three-month exchange about the problem with his mother, who had earnest suggestions as to how he and Sophie might best handle it.

Doesn't she know you can't concentrate with that racket? wrote his mother. *This is your living, for goodness sake. Your father said you could sue her for "blocking commerce," or some-such thing.*

His mother and father lived in the same Chicago neighborhood where they'd grown up. They'd bought a computer in the 1990s, used it a few times, couldn't deal with the viruses, and that was that. Sam was easily able to keep up the ruse of his and Sophie's life together.

He would cobble together fragments of his married life, and for those moments Sophie was alive and they were happy. Sophie's parents had divorced when she was young. Since Sam and Sophie had married in Paris, their parents had never met, and thus never gotten close enough to communicate. For Sam the writer, the story of Sophie being alive remained easy to tell, and comforting, if only for the time he wrote.

After he'd moved to Ville de Rachat, Sam would write the letters, put them in an envelope within an envelope, and send them to Virgile in Paris, who would then send them from a Paris postmark.

He told them he was concerned about terrorism and didn't want them to risk flying to Paris anymore. He would visit them. Then he told them Sophie could no longer fly because of a middle ear problem from a childhood infection.

Now their reunions were in New York: three days of food and drink, Broadway musicals for his mother, and Mets games for his father, a die-hard White Sox fan who couldn't bear to go to a Yankees game.

"I kinda always respected the Mets," his father would say. "Plucky, you know, Sam? You know it?"

"I know it, Pop. We always go for the underdogs."

"Maybe you should've played baseball, Sammy, natural athlete like you. You were too skinny for football. Your mom worried about you when you were playing football for Curie. Every time you tackled somebody she damn near fainted."

"That wasn't often, Pop. And I'm still healthy as a horse. Both Sophie and me."

Today, watching Ellen and Adva together, touched by their love for each other despite their disagreements, he believed his time for the kind of love they shared—that his mother and father shared—had come and gone.

Chapter Twenty

THE NEXT DAY, SAM was reading about the new release of the Côtes du Rhône when he heard a knock at his front door.

From his chair near the woodstove he saw a man, sturdy if thirty pounds overweight, clean-shaven, wearing a khaki barn jacket with a red corduroy collar and no hat on this cold day. He answered the door.

"May I help you?"

"Sam, right? We met the day you moved in."

The man moved closer. "Michael Shield? The cop?"

Sam smiled. "Of course. Come in."

Sam nodded toward the kitchen table and one of the two chairs.

"No furniture yet to speak of," he said. "Can I get you one of those Cubans? I haven't smoked any yet."

"I'll take a rain check. But thanks."

He looked around the barren kitchen.

"One more chair and you're Thoreau. At least it's toasty in here," Shield said. "Is this where you write your magazine articles?"

"Here, or the bookstore or library. It's a nice town for that. Like you said."

It was cloudy but not snowing outside. Sam said, "Coffee, wine, or tap water, I'm afraid, Sergeant." Sam held up some instant coffee.

"It's Michael or Mike, please. And you know what? It's Sunday, I'm off today, and tomorrow is New Year's Eve. I'll have a little taste of wine, if it's open. I'm guessing it's good."

"I wouldn't mind calling you Mike. Sort of reminds me of my native Chicago. Seems like half the guys I knew were called Mike."

Sam took out a Swiss Army knife and used the corkscrew to open a bottle of 2007 Côtes du Rhône Rosé Heritage des Caves des Papes.

"This is a nice afternoon wine," Sam said. "From the southern Rhone Valley. It's more for summer, but I think you'll like it. They make it near where I used to live."

"Paris?"

"I lived in a small village on the coast for a while. Sort of like this place, but different. They had a town square like you do. But not shaped like a triangle."

Mike smiled. "That's right. They . . . we . . . call it Triangle Park, or the Village Triangle. I'm not sure which is right."

"Like the pyramids in Egypt," Sam said. "Or in front of the Louvre. And in a park where I've been in Paris." Sam handed Shield his wine. "Some people believe that triangles bring creativity and harmony—lots of good things."

"Never gave it much thought," Shield said. "The coast?"

"The coast of southern France."

The sergeant didn't change his expression.

"That must have been a little boring after Paris. Or was it one of those fancy tourist places?"

"No, no," Sam said. "Very quiet and medieval. Working people mostly. My neighbors are—were—retired. Nice folks."

The sergeant picked his glass back up and examined it in the cloudy light from the window.

"Nice glasses. You bring these with you?"

"I bought a couple of them at your own Kurt's Fine Wines around the corner. I got the coffee and food there, too."

Sam stood up and opened the refrigerator. "I bought some Dutch cheese. Made with goat's milk. And decent bread."

"I'm good, thanks," Shield said. He patted his stomach. "Cholesterol. The wife. She watches me like a hawk."

Sam shut the refrigerator door.

"No problem. *À votre santé.* To your health, and Happy New Year, Sergeant. Mike."

"Cheers," Shield said.

He drank.

"This is very good."

Sam took a long drink. "It's inexpensive, too. Anyway. Glad you like it."

There was a pause as they listened to the logs crackling.

"What can I do for you? Neighbor complaints? I'm trying to quit smoking. Never should have started again."

Sam smiled and they both took another drink.

"The wife—Margie—sent me over with this."

Shield took out a crumpled envelope from the pocket of his barn coat.

"I smushed it a little on my walk over. We live down the road and up toward Whitesburg Preserve."

"I've seen the sign pointing to it," Sam said. "I plan to start walking it when the snow melts."

Michael opened the envelope and took out an invitation. There were pointed hats, noisemakers, and musical notes against a black background. Inside, handwritten, it read:

Dear Sam,

Please join the Shields for A Family New Year's Eve. Bring nothing but yourself and a hearty appetite!

Warm Regards from Amanda, Margie and Michael
Shield.

Sam stared at it for a moment too long.

"Everything okay?" Shield asked. "If you have plans . . ."

Sam swished his wine, took a sip.

"No, no. I've got nothing going on. I'm not big on parties,
though, Mike. I don't want to insult anyone."

"Not a party, Sam. Just us Shield family members. Immediate
family."

"I'd like that, Mike. Please tell . . ."

He opened the card again and read it. The thought of being
home alone or walking into the village and going to Whirly's as
Adva and Ellen had suggested—both sounded dreadful to Sam.
To be at someone's home—maybe that would be a respite from
the loneliness of staying home and of crowds.

" . . . Margie . . . that I'll be there. And I'll bring the wine,
since you like this."

Shield downed what was left of his glass, which Sam had
poured appropriately light. He stood up.

"She'll be pleased. Margie's a bit of a, well, not mother hen
. . ."

"She's a good woman, in other words," Sam said.

"Yes," Shield said. "She's got my back."

Sam walked Shield to the door. One doubt; he had to know.

"And Amanda? She's . . . ?"

"Our daughter. Home from college. It's not a set-up, Sam.
Not that you're not a nice guy, but she's a bit on the young side,"
Michael said and smiled warmly. "You're welcome to bring a
date, though."

"I'm not interested right now, Mike. Women are not on my
immediate agenda."

"Hey, whatever floats your boat. We have two ladies down the hill who are . . . that are . . . what do they call it . . . living an alternative lifestyle. Heck, I'm from New York City . . ."

"I've met them. And no, that's not why. I'm just not dating these days."

"So we'll see you, then? Around eight?" Shield said.

"Yes," Sam said. "I'll be there with . . . what's that expression? Bells on."

"With bells on. Right. I'm glad. Margie'll be glad, too." He turned and looked at Sam.

"I hope I'm not out of line. It's just that you seem really alone. Like you could use a couple of friends. Anyway, Margie can't wait to talk books with you. She's a bigger reader than me."

"I'm not much of a reader," Sam said. "More of a writer. But sure, I look forward to it. I'll fake it."

"Sounds good," Sergeant Michael Shield said. He turned and walked a few paces, then turned back to Sam, who was standing in the front doorway, breathing in the fresh, clean, cold air.

"Sam, I'll be honest here. I'll always be a New Yorker. I have friends here, sure. But I've always felt a little out of place. Maybe that's why, I don't know, I think I get you a little bit. What's French for *friend*?"

"*Ami*," Sam said.

"Well, there you go, Sam, my *ami*." He smiled. "See you tomorrow then."

"*Prends soin de toi*," Sam said back to Michael. "Take care of yourself."

Sam closed the door, walked to the kitchen and poured another glass of wine.

Chapter Twenty-One

LEE WANTED A QUIET dinner with his mother and father at Chestnut Valley Country Club. Not being members, his parents couldn't pay, even if they wanted to. Of course, the real money was at the more exclusive Pepper Pike Club, where his father belonged. But Lee couldn't stand having to deal with the powerful men who inhabited its clubhouse and fairways. Chestnut Valley Country Club was just fine with him—he could be the center of attention without having to run into his father and his friends.

As usual, he insisted that they eat anything they wanted. Money, he did not need to say, was no object. That had been the way of the Clayborne men since Father's fortunes had turned around when Lee was a teenager, when Father inherited eighteen million after-tax dollars from Grandfather. At long last Father was no longer fallen; he was redeemed.

The dinners were surf 'n turf for Father, trout almondine for Mother. Lee ordered a salmon Caesar salad for himself. He wanted his father to know he took care of his body, even if his father didn't mind his own appalling beer belly.

The wine, he had picked out the wine weeks before—a 2004 Spottswoode Estate St. Helena Cabernet Sauvignon. He did not mention the three-hundred-dollar price for the wine to his mother and father. He did not ask them how they liked it. He hardly touched his own glass, leaving a fifty-dollar pour of

Cabernet. He and the staff would know how much it cost and that was enough.

"I know I'm overdoing it with the no drinking and driving thing," he said, and grinned in his bashful way. "But I like to set an example for the younger guys in town."

His father did not look up from his steak, but he saw his mother's loving gaze.

"Village Council president. Imagine. Maybe 'Senator Clayborne' some day?" Mother smiled and nodded her head approvingly. "I'm so proud of you, Lee."

There was a large part of a second bottle left after dinner, and he took his server, Henry, aside and asked that the remainder of the wine go to the staff—this in addition to a large tip and his personal wish they have all have a Happy New Year, and his thanks for another outstanding year at the club.

His parents knew they were not to fuss over his taking them to dinner on New Year's Eve. Lee was a good son, especially to his mother. He sent her flowers for her birthday, Mother's Day, and any occasion he could think of. Lee made her laugh. She'd seen him cry only once, years ago, but from the bottom of his soul, as she held him.

Though she had stopped telling him how sad she felt for him when he was alone on New Year's Eve, Lee knew his mother grieved for him when he'd told her how he'd had his heart broken by—in his mother's words—"that lesbian."

After the divorce Mother told Lee she'd always known that the overly ambitious Indian woman was wrong for him. He didn't care how his father saw him tonight, but he knew just how his mother did. Here he was again, all these years later, still dateless, buying them an expensive dinner.

How could that woman have left him? Lee made sure she knew he took care of people in ways they never appreciated.

He'd bought Adva her lovebirds, doted on her, pampered her. He treated her like a princess, not like the slut that Mother always suspected she was.

But Lee's mother and father had no way of knowing what was on his mind this New Year's Eve. During supper, he kept his hand away from his cell phone, with its restricted outgoing number. Instead, Lee Clayborne, the culmination of generations of effort and sacrifice, attempted to give his complete and focused attention to his parents.

Lee arrived home at around ten. He changed his clothes for a two-hour workout in his finished basement. At midnight he was on the treadmill. He did not acknowledge the New Year, as was his tradition when he was without a special woman. No TV, no parties. Next year, he was sure, that woman would be Rachel, the first woman he'd met in a long time worthy of his attention. She was the one for him. That much he knew. If it hadn't been for that scumbag Johnny Kenston, he wouldn't be alone now. He despised being bossed around, much less thrown out of a fucking dump like Whirly's. Now he'd have to make up for lost time. By this time next year, he didn't want to take his parents to dinner without a date for himself. Maybe more than a date. *Rachel Clayborne* had a nice sound to it.

Chapter Twenty-Two

MARGIE SHIELD OPENED THE front door of the blue house on High Street. Sam wore a new black parka and watch cap, and the black gloves he'd received from Ellen and Adva.

"You must be Sam," Margie said. She smiled, opened the door wider, and offered her hand.

Sam shook it, then handed her two bottles of wine in a canvas sack.

"Ah, yes, the wine. Michael said you'd bring some. Good of you."

Margie took the sack and put it on the hall table.

"We're in chaos here. He had a train wreck today."

Sam stopped in the middle of taking off his parka, his hands frozen behind him.

"My God," Sam said. "Where? Is he all right?"

"Downstairs."

She nodded at the basement door.

"Oh, no. I'm sorry." She laughed. "He's fine. It's his model trains. The new locomotive jumped the track and ran off the Ping-Pong table. He's been fixing it all day. He was beside himself."

She took Sam's parka and hung it up and walked to the basement door.

"Mikey, your friend is here," she called out, then turned back to Sam. "Sam, I'm embarrassed, but Mikey couldn't remember your last name. He said he thought it was Swedish."

"It's Koppang, Mrs. Shield. Norwegian, but pretty much the same thing if you go back far enough. My father's people lived only a couple hundred kilometers from the Swedish border."

"Sit, sit, sit, Mr. Koppang." Margie urged Sam into a small, tidy living room. Photos of mother, father, and daughter were on the fireplace mantle. A 1970s white glass lamp with yellow flowers and decals of a blue butterfly shared a round table with more photos.

"Call me Sam, please. You have a lovely home. Very comfortable."

Sam sat in one of two light green wing chairs in the living room. A small fire had all but burned out. Margie took a poker and shuffled the wood coals.

"Mikey let the fire go out. I'll have him—"

"Please, let me," Sam offered. He stood, then stooped to reach into the wood recess on the side of the fireplace. He took out three pieces of well-cut, dry oak.

"This is one thing I enjoy," he said, working intently to put the three logs into a suitable configuration to catch fire from the remaining coals. He poked around and the fire caught quickly.

"There," he said, as Margie watched and nodded. "I've finally done some useful work in Chestnut Falls."

"I find that impossible to believe, Sam," Margie said. "I couldn't write for a living if you paid me. Your work is useful to someone. Of course it is!"

Sam turned and smiled as Michael, and a sort of younger female version of him entered the room.

"Good to see you, Sam. This is Mandy—Amanda—my little girl."

She stood six feet tall, like her dad, and considerably taller than her mother. Amanda shook Sam's hand. He wasn't used to young American women's handshakes and she crushed his unwary fingers.

"I'm sorry," she said, seeing him wince. "I have an overzealous grip."

She looked at her father, then her mother, and smiled.

"It's their fault," Amanda said.

"I'm fine," Sam said. "I'll be prepared next time. It's a good handshake."

Amanda laughed.

"It's nice to meet you, Sam," she said, walking toward the closet door. "I thought I was going to join you for the annual craziness here," she said and winked at her mother. "Crazy if you don't mind nodding off before midnight. But I need to be with my friend."

"I'll explain later," Michael said to Sam. He looked at Amanda. "We'll miss you, honey. You're doing the right thing. You tell Rachel if she needs anything, let us know. And you too."

Amanda left through the front door. Margie motioned to Sam to sit back down. The fire burned happily.

"Just to clear that up," Margie began, as they sat down to eat. "Amanda's got a friend—Rachel—she went to high school with. They graduated together, class of 2005, Chestnut Falls High School. Isn't that right, Mikey?"

"It's 2008 . . . so, yes, that's it," Shield said.

"She's afraid she's being . . ."

"Stalked," Michael said. "A fellow that came into the bar where she works in the village keeps calling her. She's freaked out."

"Who's the stalker?" Sam asked, his voice staying steady. It couldn't be him. Could it?

"Not sure," Margie said. "But Lord help him if Mandy gets ahold of him. She's a tough cookie."

"And she's got my number," Michael said. He fished around in his pocket, moving his girth around enough to get out a cell phone. "All she has to do is call her old man. One-touch speed dial." He smiled. "It's a great thing."

"I spend half my time trying not to worry about my husband and daughter. They're both going to give me a heart attack," Margie said.

"Honey, everything's fine," Michael said. He put his hand out and touched Margie's. She smiled at him.

"But enough of this," she said. "Tell us about what you do, Sam. Tell Mikey and me about your writing, your life. And why, for goodness sake, you're here, of all places."

Sam realized with his first bite that Margie Shield was an extraordinary cook. She'd made a simple pot roast, but one so tender and imbued with spices and vegetables that Sam couldn't discern all the flavors.

"Yes, I'm happy to talk about that. But first, Margie . . ."

He put down his fork and knife.

"This meal is absolutely wonderful. Now, then, Mike . . ."

Sam looked at his new friend and smiled. He felt a rush of affection, and with it, a tightening in his stomach—a warning to not get too close to him, or anyone.

"You live with an artist. This," he said, brushing his hands over the food, "is a work of art."

He took another bite.

Michael nodded and looked back and forth between Margie and Sam. "Yes," he said. "She's the best cook—chef—I've ever known. She could have her own restaurant. You wouldn't be able to get a reservation. *You* could. But the general public . . ."

"Did they teach you those nice manners in France, Sam? And

I thought the French were rude," Margie said. "Oh, my gosh, that was rude of *me*."

"The French can be as rude as anyone," Sam said. "But back to your food . . . This really is superb."

The talk turned to Chestnut Falls. Sam learned where the speeders sped on the side streets; that the crosswalks weren't paid much attention to by drivers or walkers; and that the police in Chestnut Falls handled about 90 percent of their problems, as Shield put it, "under the radar."

"The chief likes us to take care of our own," he said. "Sometimes that means dealing with the bad guys in ways that keep the good guys out of the line of fire. Away from lawsuits and neighbor-against-neighbor stuff, that sort of thing."

Michael spoke between mouthfuls of pot roast, mashed potatoes, a field green salad, and Margie's pecan pie, which she had made for tonight. This, too, was a Shield family tradition on New Year's Eve.

Sam could tell that Michael Shield, for all his experience, had more pride in his small-town job than he had first let on.

Sam watched Margie and Michael love each other from across a flowered tablecloth.

He could have had that love. He did have that. But it was taken from him. A man somewhere on the other side of the village took love away from him, took Sophie away.

Hours later, toward the dawn of the new year, Sam had all but forgotten the love he'd seen in two couples, both neighbors, so different, so similar, Adva and Ellen, Mike and Margie. So much love everywhere he looked, yet so much hatred covering his own heart.

Chapter Twenty-Three

RACHEL ROSEN HAD SLEPT little since her Christmas Eve encounter with Lee Clayborne at Whirly's Main Street Grill. Tonight she waited anxiously for Amanda Shield, her best friend since middle school.

Terror clenched at her gut and squeezed, almost doubling her over. *He doesn't even know me. What is going on?*

Rachel no longer wanted to drink, though this was her first legal New Year's Eve. She didn't want to let down her defenses.

Through the week, she'd tried not to check her parents' voice mail. But she needed to know what the voice on the private number that kept showing up in the caller ID display was saying. After she listened once, the private number itself began to do its work: her heart fluttered and her skin sweated.

She wondered if Lee knew her parents were out of town skiing in Jackson Hole until January 6. She wondered if he watched her. Though her father's and stepmother's gated community in the semirural suburb of South Russell had a neighborhood watch, there were too many curtainless windows for someone to peer through. Especially someone who looked liked he belonged there.

Rachel wished she had taken that apartment in Cleveland Heights, on the fourth floor, with its dirty old curtains that at least kept the world at bay. She had almost taken it, but it was too far in the winter; driving to Kent from the Heights was a nightmare of slippery hills toward Kent and traffic in the Heights. She regretted not living in a dorm at Kent State. She'd wanted to work, to make her own way, and Whirly's was here, near her parents' home. It had made sense, once, not long ago.

All week, she'd felt his eyes, even if she was quite sure he wasn't there. She recalled his voice from that night at Whirly's. It was all she could do not to run out of the house when the phone rang. But where would she go? She could lock herself in the wine cellar, but it was no use; her fear would still be there and claustrophobia would take over.

So she stayed frozen in the kitchen, near the phone and its caller ID display. She thought about his handsome face that melted in her mind into a grotesquerie. She thought about how he had looked at her body in a way that made her want to hide it, to cover it.

Finally, she listened. The twenty-six messages he'd left so far today were a variation on the first one, which he continually altered with small changes in inflections and word order.

"Hey, Rachel. Geez, this is awkward, but here goes. Lee Clayborne here. I'm calling to let you know that my intentions are all good. And that I feel like we got off to the wrong foot that night, and I totally understand if you don't want to see me. So listen: You should know that I realize I was a complete idiot. I did have the worst day of my professional life. But no excuses, right? Anyway, I'm thinking coffee and a chit-chat. I'd love to make it up to you and let you know I've got my faults, but, and I feel silly saying this: I'm a good guy. At least that's what my mom says."

Then he paused and said, *"And who the heck is going to argue with his mom, right? Anyway, talk soon."*

And then Lee Clayborne hung up, and Rachel Rosen began to shake and cry.

At last, the doorbell rang four times, with intermittent knocks on the door between rings, the agreed-upon code between the two friends. She opened the door.

When Rachel saw Amanda, tall and grinning and holding two blue plastic bags filled with beer and chips and cookies, and another white plastic bag with three chick-flick DVDs, Rachel smiled for the first time in what seemed like forever.

"Thank God you're here."

"Have you got a baseball bat?" Amanda said, as she walked to the kitchen and began putting the beer in the refrigerator.

"Why? What do you think he'll do?"

"Nothing. Oh, Rachel. Look. Bullies are mooks. They're cowards. That's what my dad says. He's dealt with his fair share. Lee Clayborne won't do anything. He probably never did anything in his whole life. He gets his rocks off intimidating a girl and then he moves on to the next one. My dad says guys like him are usually all talk. This one makes phone calls. That's his M.O."

Rachel knitted her eyebrows.

"His modus operandi. The way he does things," Amanda said. "But tomorrow we file a police report if you want."

"I don't know," Rachel said, pacing the kitchen. "A baseball bat. My dad plays softball. Maybe in the garage. I'll look. Mooks?"

"One of my dad's cop expressions." Amanda said.

Rachel walked out of the kitchen, toward the door to the garage.

"Forget the bat," Amanda said. "If he shows up, we dial 911. Cops will be here in two minutes, tops. Okay?"

Rachel reentered the kitchen and sat down. Amanda twisted the bottle caps off two beers and gave one to Rachel, who put down the beer and stared at it.

"Rach, listen. Sure, Lee Clayborne's a mook and all that. But there's something else about this guy . . ."

"What?" Rachel felt the panic rising higher, going into her throat.

"I can't say for sure. I'm not a psych major. But I've taken a class." Amanda smiled. Rachel's face froze, so Amanda went on:

"We studied personality disorders, obsession, things like that." She paused.

"Do you want to hear this?"

"What is it?" Rachel replied. "What am I dealing with? Who am I dealing with? Why me, for God's sake?"

"Look. I don't know what he has, or why, or anything, but he's a poster boy for a narcissist, maybe a sociopath, with all these phone calls. I don't know. Whatever he has, he's not normal."

"Oh my God," Rachel said. "I've got a psycho? Why does he care about me? I've met him, what . . . twice? I'm terrified."

"They fixate," Amanda continued. "They idealize. You're not the first. You won't be the last. My dad is right about that. He says he wants you, right? He tries to act charming and sweet on those creepy messages he's been leaving?"

"Yes," Rachel said, barely getting out the word as her throat constricted.

"He gets off on it, Rach."

"On what?"

"On scaring you. On getting in your head. You're his latest target."

Rachel stood up and paced. "Oh my God!" She started to shake and cry again.

"No, Rach. No. You're not a physical target. A psychological target. That's all, but that's bad enough. I'm sorry. I don't want to scare you. I just want you to understand that what he's got is probably an illness or a condition. But it's not you. You're just in his line of . . ." She trailed off, thought better of it. "I'm sure he won't hurt you."

Rachel stopped pacing, turned and looked at her best friend. It made sense.

"Do you think he'll leave me alone?"

"Yes. Soon. These guys move on."

"Really?"

"Yes, they do. They're fucked-up assholes, Rach. But the good news—I suppose—is that they soon become somebody else's fucked-up asshole. Okay?"

Rachel finally smiled.

"It's funny to hear you swear."

"Sometimes gosh and golly and gee don't cut it." Amanda smiled at her friend and put a hand on her arm as Rachel finally sat down.

Rachel knew Amanda was referring to her parents, Michael and Margie, whose old-school way of talking they'd giggled about for years.

"My dad will look out for you, Rach. If Lee Clayborne comes around here, Daddy'll take him down. He'd probably love it. He doesn't know that I know he was kind of a badass in New York."

"Really? *Your* dad was a badass?"

"Really. My dad. Can you believe it?"

They both laughed.

"It's the weirdest thing," Rachel said, staring at the beer that she still hadn't touched. "When I first met him . . ."

"What?" Amanda said.

"It's embarrassing."

"It's me, Rachel."

"Don't ever tell anyone this." She paused. "I know you won't. It's just that that guy—Lee—when I first saw him come in Johnny's place . . ."

"That night?"

"No, not that night. Another night. Before that. Johnny served him while I was making little plates. I watched him with his friends, and he was so . . . oh, God. This is sick."

"He was so . . . ?" Amanda said.

"Charming. Funny. I thought, 'He's good-looking; he works out; he takes care of himself; he has a really nice smile.' I mean, I think I might have smiled at him. He seemed so normal. He was telling his friends jokes—I remember this—and they were laughing their heads off, and I wanted to be a part of it. He seemed really cool."

"That's part of it, Rach," Amanda said. "You know that now, right? These guys can charm your pants off. Not yours, but—"

"How could I have been so wrong?" Rachel said. "This whole thing has made me doubt myself. It's made me wonder if *I'm* crazy."

Chapter Twenty-Four

BRIGHT DECEMBER TURNED TO dark and icy January. Clouds were low and weary. Residents of Chestnut Falls generally left one another alone. Store owners took inventory and sold off their goods at discounts or worked fewer hours.

Bartenders served only regulars and the occasional business-person passing through.

The village's Christmas lights stayed on long after the holiday had been reduced to photographs and bills, to memories of family longed for or relieved of, remembrances of celebratory elation and crushing loneliness.

During one of his walks through the gray slush and cinders on the sidewalks and streets of Chestnut Falls, Sam Koppang decided it was time to look his demon in the face.

Chapter Twenty-Five

By EARLY FEBRUARY, SAM had developed the habit of reading the local paper, which came out every Thursday, at the library, a block and a half from his house. The *Chestnut Valley Times* fascinated him, with its stories about the village—art exhibits, zoning arguments, dog bites and domestic fights, full coverage of every high school athletic team in the Chestnut Valley, boys and girls. He read the editorials and the columnists, the police blotter, and page after page of letters to the editor. So many people passionate about everything from trees being cut down by the electric company whether a mural on a building constituted an illegal sign, to long citizen letters to the editor that covered every end of the political spectrum.

He read each word about Village Council president Lee Clayborne closely, always more than once. And he saw in the classifieds a window into the collective life of an American village and its surrounding towns. So different from Ville de Rachat, yet so similar, but for one glaring thing: People in America seemed to need to get rid of or acquire a lot of things.

Then one day, he saw a classified for an office rental on Main Street. He folded the newspaper and put it back on the wooden slats and headed out of the library, wearing in his warm gifts from Adva and Ellen.

As Sam turned left from Orange Street onto Main and walked fifty feet, he saw a sign, written in black marker on a piece of corrugated box that was taped to the inside window of the Chestnut Valley Hardware Store: "Second-Floor Offices for Rent—Inquire Within."

He looked up. If the available office sat in the front section of the building, the window would face the Town Hall, directly across Main Street. If that were so, he could see the comings and goings of the Village Council on the third Thursday evening of each month. He'd seen one photo of Lee Clayborne in the *Times*. He would recognize him. Now he could watch an unaware Lee Clayborne on his own terms.

He looked up at the window of the office in question. He imagined himself, like a sniper, pointing a rifle through that window down at the street below. Could he do that? He'd never held a gun—he hadn't lied to Ellen. Yet something like sexual desire hit his groin and stomach. He wanted to learn to shoot, to kill Lee Clayborne with a rifle, put a bullet through his rancid brain.

Sam walked inside the hardware store.

Sam had come to know Jimmy Schultz, the owner of the Chestnut Falls dual-duty institution—hardware store and ministry of information for the townspeople.

James Sr. had retired fifteen years earlier and now lived in Arizona. Jimmy ran the store alone.

Sam had avoided striking up a friendship with Jimmy when he stopped in for items for the house, but he enjoyed their conversations as he browsed the odd antiques and knickknacks that were mixed in with hardware supplies: lead soldiers displayed next to the paint section; old kerosene lamps and vintage Beatles posters lined up next to fasteners and screwdrivers.

Jimmy Schultz, like Johnny Kenston, knew the town's business but kept the serious information to himself. If a story was funny and no one would get hurt by a bit of gossip, it was fair game. Otherwise, Jimmy's information vault stayed locked.

Fifty-seven years old, Jimmy was well versed in European and Middle Eastern affairs and provided a good conversational distraction for Sam on the days he didn't want to think or write about wine and couldn't stop thinking about Sophie.

One day in February, Sam and Jimmy spoke of the Iraq war, then of Iran, where Jimmy had lived for two years in the 1970s, as part of his college education, back when he'd wanted to be a diplomat. He'd seen the shah of Iran begin his fall from grace and his throne. Jimmy spoke of the Persian people with admiration and disappointment at their place in the world in 2008.

"It's a beautiful culture," Jimmy said. "I hate to see what's going on."

When the conversation dwindled and the afternoon sunlight filtered through the dust, Sam asked about the offices for rent.

Jimmy told Sam the rent was six hundred dollars a month for the large office and three hundred for the small. Sam asked to see the small office.

The south wall of the office was exposed brick. Each brick weathered differently: some had edges gone to powder, some jutted out like shale on a glaciated riverbed. In the middle of the office was a hand-hewn post from the building's 1850s construction, blackened with age from the coal furnace that had burned when the building was a Masonic Temple.

"Someday I'll show you the third floor, where the Masons held their meetings," Jimmy said, as they made their way down the steep, shallow, worn stairway from the second-floor office. "If you like that sort of thing. Watch yourself here. Use the railing."

Sam made his decision.

Jimmy didn't ask why Sam wanted an office. He knew Sam was a writer and that sometimes writers needed a solitary space. He'd seen and known too many folks who lived alone to question their motives about anything. And he didn't question when Sam told him he'd be right back.

Sam walked up the hill and into his house. Fifteen minutes later he walked back down the hill and into Chestnut Valley Hardware. He took nine hundred dollars in cash out of his wallet and laid it down on the counter. Jimmy looked up and over his half glasses. He counted the money and handed three hundred back to Sam. He took a receipt pad from the counter and wrote, "$600.00. First and last month's rent. Suite 2."

"Give me a few days to clean it up," he told Sam. "Go over there," he nodded in the direction of the cleaning supplies and paper products, "and grab thirty dollars' worth of stuff you can use at your house."

"Why?"

Jimmy tapped the wall calendar behind the counter.

"For keeping you out of your office for three days, since you're not renting the first through the third; you'll be in on the fourth. Let's just keep it even. Isn't there anything you can use here? Or if you want, I can write you a check for the three days."

"There's almost nothing I can't use," Sam said. "I'll pick it up over the next couple of days, okay?"

"Whatever works for you," Jimmy said.

The two men shook hands.

"I think you'll like the view," he said. "With the Town Hall, Whirly's, and the new Asian place opening next to it, you'll have a decent view of comings and goings."

Jimmy went back to his ledger. Sam looked down and saw him write, "Received from Sam."

"I don't know your last name," Jimmy said.

"Koppang," Sam said, and spelled it.

Without looking up, Jimmy said, "That's a village in Norway. In the mountains, right? Did your family come from there? I know the Norwegians sometimes took their names from villages."

"You're the first person who ever knew that outside of my family."

"I get one right now and then. I like geography. Spent a month in Bergen. Rained most of the time, but it was fun."

"I've been there. Bergen, Oslo, all around."

"Tell me about it sometime," Jimmy said. "When you get settled in."

Sam thought of Norway and his honeymoon and his stomach tightened and he could barely breathe, so he simply nodded yes. He knocked twice on the counter, gave a thumbs-up sign to Jimmy, and turned to walk away, hoping to make it to the cold air before the panic attack took him.

"Sam?"

Sam turned around.

"Make your Norskie grandpa proud. Write some good stuff up there." Jimmy nodded upwards.

Sam felt dizzy, kept moving toward the front door.

"And thanks," Jimmy said.

But by then Sam had reached the street. He stumbled down Main and rounded the corner onto Orange Street, where, should Jimmy go out the front door, he wouldn't see Sam.

Sam's legs gave out and his knees hit the ground. He put his hands, in his black leather Christmas gloves, on the salt-covered sidewalk. He slowly staggered to his feet, made it up Grove Hill, opened the unlocked door of his house, and lay on his couch until the sky was dark.

Chapter Twenty-Six

SAM HADN'T VISITED THE other bars in town. He liked that Johnny left him alone. Today he was the only one in the place.

Johnny played music on his iPod hookup—Tony Bennett, John Coltrane, Ella Fitzgerald, Bob Dylan, Marvin Gaye. Sam had heard the same songs rotate over the past couple of months and barely noticed them.

Crouched down, stacking imported and domestic craft brewed beers in the cooler behind the bar, over a Sinatra tune, Johnny sensed Sam was unusually somber today.

"You can talk about her, you know," he said, without turning around.

"Talk about who?"

"Whoever she is."

A pause. Sinatra sang, "A Summer Wind."

"Whoever she was," Sam said.

"I thought that might be the case." Johnny kept stacking.

"Why?"

Johnny got up and turned around. He inhaled and breathed out through his nose, his hands on his hips.

"Men after breakups don't act the way you do."

"How do they act?"

"Pissed off. Hurt. Indignant. Guilty. Or like victims. They hit on women. They tell sad stories. They cry. They laugh and talk too loud. They throw punches. They try for sympathy."

He paused and looked out the window.

"Some men who have lost a woman make a new version of themselves. They buy things and make sure everybody knows what they bought. New car. New watch. New haircut. I knew a guy who bought a new house, a new dog, a new car, a new watch, and a new wardrobe. And that's just what he talked about in here."

He looked at Sam and laughed softly.

"For all I know the brother bought a new woman, too."

Sam tried to smile at Johnny's joke. Johnny saw it didn't work. He walked to the cash register, which faced the street. He looked at the parking spaces in front of Whirly's.

"You ever notice how many Benzes and Saabs and Jags show up here? Seems like a new one every day. Who do you think drives those things? Celebrities? Naw-uh."

Johnny turned around and opened the compartments beneath the counter that were filled with different cheeses, meats, pâtés, breads, and fruits. The grill for the Whirly Burgers was in the kitchen. Out here, in sight of the clientele, was where he put the food for those trying to impress clients, dates, each other. Tonight was Wednesday. A few regulars would be in, but the businesspeople staying at the Chestnut Inn around the corner might come in, and they'd spend money. He needed a dozen cheese, fruit, and pâté plates ready to go.

The customers' accents could be French, German, Japanese, Russian, Spanish, Irish, English, or Chinese, as well as from all over the United States.

Though they tended to be a bit loud when they drank, Johnny liked the Brits. His late father's best friend, Hugo, a bar owner from The Camp, had taught Johnny about the business when Johnny hung out there back in the 1970s. Of mixed race, Hugo was assigned to fight with the British in World War II.

"They had their tea every day, but then they fought like savages," Hugo had told Johnny. "They were the meanest fighters you ever saw. They taught me you cannot be merciful out there. You've got to kill them before they kill you."

Johnny had remembered Hugo's admonishment when he went to Vietnam. But Hugo had only killed soldiers. When Johnny came across a village and the lieutenant gave his orders, Johnny did what he was told: shot at everything that moved.

After fifteen tortured years back in the States, Johnny sought help through the VA. He got some therapy. He quit drinking, which had sent him into the dark places too often. He functioned, but the crippling guilt continued.

Then one day, around the time he turned fifty-four, six years earlier, Johnny Kenston forgave himself.

He didn't know why, and he didn't know how. But he knew when.

He was watching the second tower of the World Trade Center go down when he realized that people made deadly mistakes. Not the people who were committing the crime, who knew what they were doing. They succeeded.

It was someone else. Whoever was supposed to be minding the store. The military. The politicians. One person, ten people, thousands of people; Johnny didn't think anyone would ever know who screwed up. But someone, or maybe many people, had made horrible mistakes.

And as the towers fell, Johnny Kenston forgave himself.

Looking at Sam, he thought, this guy is not forgiving someone. Or himself.

"No," Johnny said. "Those aren't celebrities in the sixty-thousand-dollar cars. Those are guys with something to prove. Guys with a hole in their guts."

He leaned down on his elbows, but down the bar a bit, not too close to Sam.

"But not you. You don't care about proving anything to anybody. Right? You don't have to answer because I already know."

Johnny refilled Sam's glass of 2001 Coudoulet de Beaucastel Côtes du Rhône—one of Johnny's better wines, one he reserved for people who would appreciate it. Sam sniffed it again, swirled it again, tasted it again. He suddenly missed France. He closed his eyes and savored.

Johnny poured a small amount in another glass and sniffed it. "It's elegant. It takes you somewhere else, doesn't it?"

Johnny poured his taste of wine down the sink. He walked to the front door and locked it. Then he walked behind the bar, put plastic wrap on the little plates he'd prepared, and stacked them in the refrigerator.

"These'll hold," he said out loud to himself.

He walked back and sat on a bar stool one down from Sam, leaving a comfortable space between the two damaged men.

"If you want to talk about her, I'm here," Johnny said.

Chapter Twenty-Seven

"WHEN I MET SOPHIE I was a struggling writer in Paris by way of Chicago. I knew more about Leinenkugel's and Old Milwaukee than Bordeaux and Burgundies. What I knew about wine you could have put in a box. Literally put in a box with a spout on it."

This time it was Sam's turn to try a joke. Johnny laughed softly.

"What took you to Paris? That's a long way from Chi-Town," Johnny said.

"I was there for years before I met Sophie. I only knew I wanted to get away—from Chicago, from my job on the city desk at the *Tribune* that was going nowhere, from a failed marriage. I was a nobody who had married a society girl I barely knew. Chalk it off to youth, I suppose. She was outgoing, I wasn't. Maybe I thought she made up for that part of me. That was my first mistake. Anyway we were divorced within a year. I was twenty-seven years old and felt washed up.

"So I moved to Paris. I didn't speak French, but I thought I'd rather struggle there than in my hometown. Not that I thought there was anything special about Paris. I never bought the Hemingway crap."

He paused and looked around, as if expecting to see someone. "Well, maybe a little bit. So I rented a tiny flat I found in the northwest corner of the city. There was a place nearby called

Café Virgile that catered to artists and writers, mostly unsuccessful and unpublished. I met a few fellow expatriates. They were usually guys with money who sat and drank and talked all day. I started editing their manuscripts for a fee. I can't tell you how many budding and wilting Hemingways and Fitzgeralds I met. None of them were particularly publishable, but these guys wanted to hope, so I gave them some hope. At least that's how I justified taking their money.

"I wanted to write my own stuff, but I didn't know what to write. I started learning a little about wine from Virgile, who became my friend. But professionally, it wasn't happening. I couldn't get a writing gig, and I was running out of money.

"Then I met Sophie. She sold wine for a big distributor. Café Virgile was one of her customers. Virgile introduced us.

"I looked at her and fell in love. She later said she did too. That happens, Johnny. I mean, it happened once. To me. And to her."

"I believe you."

"The only difference—one I'll always regret—is that she showed it more than I did at first. I was defensive. Eventually I came around and let her know how I felt. We moved in together. With her encouragement, I wrote a spec book on wine—it was for English speakers in Europe, but was mostly about French wine. A little book, not a big deal, but it caught on enough to get me a column in the magazine I write for now. She helped me. I mean, I couldn't have written it without her. But she didn't want any credit. She just wanted me to be happy. She was the best person I ever met, Johnny. Selfless, kind, beautiful . . .

"We started making some money—with my book selling in the UK and the States and a little bit elsewhere and her job, we started traveling. But she didn't want to give up our little apartment. 'Too many happy memories,' she said. 'Let's make a baby. I want to raise a baby in this apartment,' she'd say. In that little hole in the wall."

Johnny stayed quiet while Sam was lost in thought.

"Sophie loved it when it rained in Paris. She loved the sound of it, loved the feel of it through the windows. We lived over an East African restaurant. I remember the music and the smells . . ."

Sam stopped again, lost somewhere in the northwest corner of Paris, at his and Sophie's flat. Johnny sat for a few minutes. He got up and poured Sam some more Côtes du Rhône.

"We got married at a place called le parc Monceau. The marriage was legal, but the ceremony probably wasn't. We didn't have a permit for the park. We hired a friend of Virgile's, some fallen priest from Normandy, and we got married quickly under a huge tree. Then all of us—Sophie and me, Virgile, the priest, and some drunk who showed up and watched the ceremony, crying his eyes out the whole time—went back to the café.

"Johnny, it was *so simple*. But it was the greatest day of my life. Then again, they were all like that with Sophie. I never knew—"

Sam stopped as they both listed to Edith Piaf sing "Hymne à L'Amour"—"Hymn to Love"—the song that Piaf wrote the wrenching lyric to when her lover died in a plane crash on his way to see her perform. Sam knew the story, Johnny sensed it, so the two men didn't speak until it was over and Herbie Hancock began playing "Maiden Voyage."

"You never knew what?" Johnny finally continued.

Sam wanted to say, *That she was diseased because of a rape and beating by someone in this town.* Instead he said, "That she would get so sick. And when she got sick, I never thought she'd die."

Johnny put his hand on Sam's shoulder.

"What are you doing here, brother? In Chestnut Falls, of all places. How long has it been?"

"Since she died? Five years. I spent nearly all of that time in the south of France. I couldn't handle Paris without her. It became a sad place, nothing like it was when she was alive. So I moved into Virgile's family cottage. He never used it. I had sort of a life there. Solitary. But a life. I had a couple of friends and my work. I had a cat."

The wine had gone to Sam's head and he became afraid he'd said too much.

"What are you doing here, Sam?" Johnny said.

Sam turned to Johnny. He shook his head slowly back and forth. Then he looked down.

Finally Johnny said, "I learned after the army, after Nam, that some questions should be answered but can't be. I hope this isn't one of those times. Is it?"

"I need to come to terms with something."

"Something or someone, Sam?"

"I don't want to lie to you, Johnny. So I won't."

Sam slowly put on his coat. He put down his money. Johnny gave it back to him.

"Not tonight, Sam. Consider it a talk between two old friends. I'm filling in for Virgile. Okay?"

"I owe you, Johnny."

"No, no," Johnny said. "We're just two guys in a foxhole. And Sam? Think about what she'd want for you. Okay?"

Sam and Johnny shook hands. Sam walked out the door and headed up the hill.

Chapter Twenty-Eight

SAM TURNED IN HIS rental car in early February. A woman from the agency drove him back to Chestnut Falls and dropped him off at the hardware store.

Sam hand-delivered a fifteen-hundred-dollar money order made out to Jimmy Schultz for a blue, no-frills 1989 Chevy pickup, which Jimmy had been using as backup for his 2000 Ford Bronco.

"It's not exactly a show truck," Jimmy said. "The heater and the radio work. Beyond that, it's basic transportation. I hope you're not planning on impressing any dates with it."

Jimmy patted the roof of the truck. He glanced sideways at Sam and gave him a small, closed-mouth smile. He had thinning sandy hair and was still trim. Slightly stooped, he emanated world-weariness. His was a hard business. Day in and day out, he and two employees unloaded trucks early in the morning, mixed paint, found obscure parts for old appliances, fixed screen doors in the summer and storm doors in the winter. Jimmy did his own books on the weekends.

"Strange transportation for a writer. Don't you guys drive old Volvos or hybrids? What do you want with a beat-up pickup truck?"

He paused, glanced sideways. Sam noticed that Jimmy tended to look at people as if through some kind of lens above his reading glasses, almost as if he was looking into the person.

"Don't you write about wine?"

"I'm trying to keep my money local," Sam said. "I like doing business with people I know. It's a habit from the little town where I lived in France."

Jimmy looked out toward the street. "I see you walking every day. You're not one of those guys stuck in The Bubble, are you? There are people here who haven't been out of this town in decades."

"I drove to the mountains a couple of times."

Jimmy snapped his head around and looked at Sam.

"Mountains?"

"The Alleghenies. I drive out to Pennsylvania. They're not so far. It's a nice drive."

"No kidding. You hunt? That's *Deer Hunter* country up there. 'One shot.' I love that movie. They filmed part of it in Cleveland." He paused and looked at Sam. He gave him a full smile for the first time. "De Niro. What an actor. And Christopher Walken . . ."

"I drive out and talk wine and sports with the guy who runs a little store up in the mountains. I'm teaching him a little about wine. He's picked it up well—faster than I did in Paris, in fact."

"Huh," Jimmy said. "To each his peach. Anyway, this truck will get you where you want to go. Change the oil every few thousand miles and all that. I assume you know the drill."

"I owned a car years ago in Chicago. I'm looking forward to it."

Sam didn't ask, but Jimmy told him, as they walked from the parking lot out back into the hardware store and up to Sam's office, "I'm selling everything I can. I've got one more kid to put through college. Otherwise I'd never get rid of my stuff."

"If you reconsider, that's no problem," Sam said. "Really. Life's too short."

"Oh, no," Jimmy said. "Everything must go. Desks, bedroom furniture, lamps, you name it."

They walked down the dim, narrow, high-ceilinged hallway from Sam's office to a room full of used furniture. The room, which had a doorway onto a tar paper rooftop overlooking the east end of the village, had peeling, stained, white, faux-brick wallpaper with black, evenly spaced fleur-de-lis as a pattern.

"In your honor," Jimmy said, nodding at the fleur-de-lis.

"Some wallpaper," Sam said.

"It's atrocious, I know. A former tenant thought this was fashionable, I suppose."

Sam looked around: an antique hand-driven washing machine, a framed World War I poster, a 1950s-era rocking horse, an old wooden sled on a green and white Formica kitchen table, two rocking chairs, two unmatched end tables, and one glass-top and one wood dining room table.

Sam bought a used desk, a used leather office chair that leaned to the right, and a ladder-back, wicker-bottomed chair, in the unlikely event anyone came to visit.

Sam looked at the tags and paid cash for the asking price. Jimmy and Sam carried the furniture down the second-floor hallway and put it in Sam's new office.

There was a single window in the office. After Jimmy left, Sam placed his desk to face it, so that he had a good view of the street and the Town Hall. He'd read through the history of the village on one of his long days at the library.

First built in 1848 by Aristarchus Champion, the same Yalie who built Adva and Ellen's house, the Town Hall was originally Champion's library. Throughout the years it had been an opera house, a place to care for the poor during the Depression, and a community center. Renovated as an official village government building in 1983, the Town Hall—really the Village Hall, but the name had stuck—became the center of the village's political activity.

Now Sam had a clear view of the Italianate brick building with the large weather vane on top. He had read in the *Chestnut Valley Times* that the Village Council held its meetings on the third Thursday of each month. Sam sat in his worn leather chair behind his battered desk and watched the bundled-up people walk back and forth in front of the Town Hall and wondered what he would do when Lee Clayborne finally entered his sight.

Chapter Twenty-Nine

IT WAS THE WORLD the way he wanted it. A small town, the trees spaced just so, the buildings pleasing to his eye, none too tall, none out of place. Bricks mixed with wood, and each structure—the hardware store, the ice-cream shop, the pharmacy, the new train station, the bandstand in the middle of town, the restaurants with their folksy names, the churches with their steeples to heaven—was a brushstroke in a small masterpiece of an America in which he believed and now lived.

A river ran through the center of the village, a river from somewhere that flowed to everywhere. There were tidy buildings, most with golden lights in the windows that turned on at dusk, as if by magic. The sidewalks were neat and there were flower boxes from the spring through the autumn and Christmas lights from November through February. Only in March and part of April was the village not very beautiful, but only merely fine and calm, as if those two months were simply a breath in the middle of an aria. The village was in a valley and the valley was in a place where no one lied, no one stole, no one cheated, no one mourned for dead friends or worried about husbands or wives, sisters or brothers, sons or daughters.

Even the sounds of the place were sweet. He always heard his favorite music, the old tunes, the fifties and sixties hits that he could sing along to. This was music when there was melody, and singers sang of wanting love, needing love, finding love, losing love. The songs resolved the loves or allowed them to gently fade away.

His town smelled of perfumed cigar smoke and roasting chicken and baking pies and homemade spaghetti sauce with lots of garlic that was chopped and minced carefully, each stroke of the knife an act of devotion.

Small as it was, the village spread out as a world all its own. To him, everything in it, even the run-down old train depot, or the broken fence along a street running out of town, or the dog off the leash, was a part of its perfection.

Accidents happened, even when he took precautions. Sometimes, in the outside world, accidents mixed with malevolence. At least here, he told himself, accidents were only accidents. At least here there was no malevolence. "A hate-free zone," he called it, but only to the denizens. Yet they could not hear him.

He tried, minute by detailed and carefully crafted minute, to set things up so that there would be no accidents; yet he had long ago learned that he was not the ultimate lord of all life. He learned that in New York, when Danny Wu shot him four times in the leg and opened his femoral artery and he nearly bled to death, then Danny's gun jammed, and he emptied his 9mm into Danny Wu.

Here in the golden village he could not be farther from Danny Wu or predators like him. Here he would not be ambushed. Here was where he kept everyone—especially his wife and daughter—safe. Here was where, when accidents happened, no one died.

On the streets of this place he loved so well, people passed each other by and said hello and looked each other in the eye. They all smiled, or at least it seemed that way to Sergeant Michael Shield, here in his basement, where the trains on the table clicked and clacked and life was the way it should be.

Chapter Thirty

"HOWDY, STRANGER."

Adva swung open the front door of the Cottage Street house. When Sam entered, Ringo sniffed and licked his hand. He trotted out of the living room and into the kitchen.

"Good judge of character," Adva said, nodding to Ringo.

Sam held out two bottles of 2005 white Bordeaux, Château Haut Mallet.

"It seems like a long time. I'm sorry if you two thought I was avoiding you. Consider these an apology. At least they should go well with the pasta."

"We left a note *on a boy's door*," Adva said. "Can you imagine? Making us act like teenagers?" She considered him. "A man without a cell phone or e-mail. How are we supposed to get a hold of you? We wondered if you were just going to love and leave us. What have you been up to all of January?"

"Writing and walking. Walking and writing. I rented an office. Over the hardware store."

"That's it?" Adva said. "No dates? No friends? Nothing?"

"I go to the library?"

"Oh, Sam, please. Really?"

"Okay. I'm not a complete loner. I've made friends with a local policeman. We . . ." Sam realized he couldn't think of the American expression, then remembered. "We hung out. Drank some beer, watched a little basketball, Knicks against the

Cavaliers. I was hoping to see the Bulls, my old home team . . . but . . . anyway it was fun."

"Okay," Adva said. "That's a start."

Ellen was making a salad. Water boiled in a red ceramic pot on the stove and a fire burned in the fireplace. Sam looked through the sliding glass door out to the deck and then past it, where the snow covered the ivy on the hill that led up to his house. Jazz piano played on the stereo. Sam sank into the chair by the fireplace. McCoy Tyner played "My One and Only Love." He closed his eyes. Sophie had loved this song, had listened to it at Café Virgile. They'd listened to Tyner's syncopations and runs up and down the piano, to his countermelodies tumbling into each other and into the saxophone.

"I'm cooking again in your honor, I'll have you know, mister. A few minutes on the pasta. What's this?" Ellen said. She picked up the wine and put it on ice. "Whatever it is I can't wait to drink it."

She looked at Adva, who said to Ellen, "I know: 'Save it for dinner.'"

Ellen went to the liquor cabinet on the other side of the country kitchen and bent down. She looked around and smiled at Sam.

"So, Sam made friends with the policeman, Ellen," Adva said.

"I knew that."

"What do you mean, you knew that? Why didn't you tell me?"

"Hey, Adva. Easy. I see Mike Shield around town. We talk. He's the one who told me about Sam in the first place. I have conversations with people, dear. I don't report every one."

"Hmm. Odd. But okay," Adva said, looking at Ellen and knitting her brow.

Sam studied Adva's face. Her eyes—so brown and liquid, like a deep pool, he thought. He thought she caught him staring.

"A cocktail first? What'll you have?" Adva asked him.

Halfway through supper, Ellen said, "You've been asked this a thousand times, but I have to know."

"Oh, no," Adva said. "Here we go."

"No, wait. I need to ask him this."

"Please," Sam said. "Go ahead."

Ellen's pasta sauce was full of peppers, garlic, goat cheese, fresh basil, marjoram, and ingredients Sam couldn't place. The room smelled of Europe to him, of home. He felt as if he were in Ville de Rachat. It was late at night, when the stars spoke to him through the haze of wine, and the ache was covered, as if by a soft blanket to be thrown off the next morning.

"Tell us about wine. How you write about it. Why you write about it. It's very cool that you make your living doing that," Ellen said.

She looked at Adva.

"I mean, isn't that amazing? I think it's amazing."

"It's amazing," Adva said. "So, Sam. Talk."

In the warmth of the room, a fire crackled and outside March snow fell on early-blooming daffodils that were scattered throughout the dormant ivy on the hill. Three days of late-February weather in the high fifties had fooled the daffodils. Sam looked to his left, out the sliding glass door, and wondered if the daffodils would survive the cold.

"I'm not much of a technical writer about wine. My writing is really a kind of essay—stream of consciousness stuff, Impressionistic maybe."

Ellen nodded. "That is cool. Okay, so you're like an art critic."

"I wouldn't say that, just a wine writer who learned from a very good teacher. Sophie knew wine . . ."

He held his glass up, and looked at it for a few seconds.

"I don't want to give the wrong impression. Wine is, in some ways, quite technical, the way the grapes are grown and harvested and fermented and bottled—all of it is fine and minute when done correctly. Yet still an art more than a science. So how can I say this? A good wine is much more than the sum of its parts."

"That's the stuff I don't get," Adva said. "I go to wine tastings and I have no idea what they're talking about. I hear 'tannins' and 'finish' and 'blackberries and currant and spicy oak,' and I don't know what the hell anyone is talking about."

"Her excuse to get a little tipsy," Ellen said. "At that last tasting we went to she had a few sips, then said, 'Just fill it up and keep it coming.'"

"I don't think that went over well," Adva said.

"Okay. No tannins, no oak," Sam said. "But I'll try."

He looked around the room and out the back door as if searching for ingredients.

"There are maybe five hundred or so chemical compounds in wine that are also in other things. Such as blackberries or the odd thing like horse sweat. Usually good things, though, from grasses to honey to pears to perfume in whites; and pepper or chocolate or loamy earth to all kinds of spices in red. Nearly anything you imagine tasting or smelling can be found in wine somewhere. Honestly everything. I suppose that's what I find most fascinating. Why I keep writing about it."

He looked at the daffodils.

"Take those flowers," he said.

Adva's and Ellen's heads turned right. They focused on the yellow that they could still see through the heavy, wet snow.

"Something makes them smell the way they do. Feel the way they do. Close your eyes and imagine the feel and smell of a daffodil."

The women closed their eyes. Ellen said, "Oh, spring. Please come soon."

"Yes, spring," Sam said. "You think of spring, because you can smell and feel and see the flowers in your senses—even now. The chemicals in those flowers make them smell and feel and taste like spring. They play with your head, inside your senses, and a daffodil becomes more than a flower. It becomes an experience. A memory. Think of daffodils in your life, throughout your life, and what they mean to you, what they've meant."

"Okay," Ellen said and opened her eyes. "And?"

"That's wine."

"What's wine?"

"When done well, everything that grapes can become, from the sun, the rain, the *terroir*—the land, the rocks, the various elements of the soil—is what makes the wine what it is."

He took a sip of the white Bordeaux.

"You taste wine with all your senses. Of course, I guzzle it sometimes, like some do."

"Like me," Adva said. "Ellen says I drink it like juice."

"It is juice, really," Sam said. "Fermented juice."

"Not all the time," Ellen said. "Just when you get excited or upset."

"I'm embarrassed to admit that when I listen to people at wine tastings sometimes I want to scream," Adva said.

"And by the way, guzzle away. That's fine, if that's what you want to do," Sam said. "But you should also know that someone—and this is not always true—but usually someone put his or her heart, or their hearts into the vine that produced that wine that you and I may guzzle. That's the best case. The worst is when it's factory farmed, mass-produced, with marketing an interesting label as its prime directive—its label, its promotion, the public-relations-driven word-of-mouth campaigns that make it popular."

Sam looked outside again at the daffodils. He thought of Sophie, of what she had taught him.

"The worst of it is if the wine has no soul. Ironically even shabby, cheap little wines can have a lot of soul."

Once again there was silence in the room but for the fireplace. Sam took a deep breath.

"It's been a very long time since I talked about this with any enthusiasm," he said.

"Then we're honored," Ellen said.

"It's I who am honored," Sam said. He laughed. "I just sounded like an ass, didn't I?"

"No," Adva said. "It's good to honor one another."

"Well," Sam said. "Thank you. So . . . soul in wine. There are times when I taste a wine and it can be a wine from anywhere. The wine might be 'important' in some way—a highly anticipated vintage, say, or it received wondrous ratings from other wine writers. Then I taste it . . . and for me there's something wrong, something off, something missing. Yet the wine is delicious. So that's what I'll say: 'This wine is delicious.' That will usually get me off the hook. I don't want to offend anyone if I'm not writing about a wine, particularly a host who is giving me his finest wine, or what he believes to be his finest wine."

"What's wrong with delicious?" Ellen asked.

"Chocolate cake from a box can be delicious if you're hungry and you love chocolate and sugar. Lots of things taste delicious. But they don't necessarily have a soul or a voice. They have ingredients. They don't have the soul of the land, the grapes, the winemaker in them.

"This is simply the way I look at it. There's no right or wrong. For me, though, good wine has some soul, great wine a lot. Sometimes an inexpensive wine from a tiny vineyard will speak to me. It'll tell me where it's been, how the rains fell, how intensely the sun shone on it, how it was aged. There are times I imagine whether the vintner and his wife argued or made love, or if someone died, or a baby was born. The wine—if the wine and I are both at our best—will tell me how it was treated and what it experienced before I tasted it."

He paused. They were silent.

The fire had died down to a few small flames.

"So now you know: I'm quite mad. That probably sounded ridiculous."

Sam hoped they would laugh, but neither woman laughed.

"Not ridiculous. Are you at your best now, Sam?" Adva said. He didn't answer. Smiled tightly, shook his head no.

"You and Sophie drank wine together, didn't you?" Adva said. "She shared your passion for it."

"More than shared. She taught me. Her clients loved her, the vintners loved her because she cared so much. Sophie knew more about wine than anyone I've ever known, any writer I've read. More than the vintners, because they are so focused on their *appellations*, their *châteaux*, their Cru Classé, their wineries. She forgot far more than I will ever know."

Ellen got up and put a couple of logs on the fireplace. Adva, who had tears in her eyes, sniffed, and said, "I'm going to try not to guzzle."

Finally the three of them laughed at the same time.

After dinner, sitting in front of the fire, Sam said, "Ellen. Tell me about your hobby."

"Shooting?"

"Interesting hobby for a sculptor."

There was a loud pop in the fireplace, and they all started and laughed together again.

"Maybe that's a sign," Adva said. "You should take Sam to target practice. Get him out of the house."

"And off the street," Sam said. "I'm sure half the store owners think I'm crazy. I have a walking route that takes me up past Whitesburg's pond and then back through town. I hardly buy anything and they keep looking out their windows. I've started waving at them."

"You're trying out for village idiot, in other words," Adva said. "That's good. We need one of those. The village is too well behaved."

The panic rose in Sam—*not all well behaved*, he thought. Sam cleared his throat.

"You okay, Sam?" Ellen said as she gathered up the plates and put them in the sink.

The thoughts raced through his mind again: *Assassin. Murderer.*

"It's not something you'd be interested in, is it, Sam? My father taught me; I've been shooting since I was a kid. Shooting isn't something I'd pick up as an adult."

She turned around as she rinsed the plates, giving Sam a chance to collect himself.

"It is fun, though. You'd be surprised who goes to target ranges."

"I don't have any hobbies around here," Sam said. "I was thinking maybe mah-jongg or dominoes up at the retirement community up past Whitesburg. Did I tell you I wandered in there to use a restroom on one of my walks? I ended up staying for an hour or so. Some woman was giving a lecture on 'Bioethics in the Twenty-First Century.' It was thirty older folks and me. The pathetic part was I was the only one who fell asleep."

"Some of those older folks are livelier than we are," Adva said. "I go to a yoga class there. And by the way, have you tried mah-jongg? It's ancient, it's difficult, and I don't have the patience for it."

"She's a hit with the widowers," Ellen said, sitting back down. She took Adva's hand and stroked it. "I tell her if she leaves me for a man, it'll be one over seventy-five."

"It can't be easy, especially when they're alone. Some of them still have steam in their kettles," Adva said, catching Sam's eyes and glancing quickly away.

"Only two options: aging and death," Ellen said. "Neither one's terrific."

"Aging is better," Sam said. "Unless you're left behind."

"No, Sam," Adva said. "Aging is better. For everyone. Including those left behind. Including you."

She studied Sam's face.

"What did you do in France?" she asked. "For hobbies. The past few years, I mean."

The CD had finished playing and there was quiet but for their talking.

"Since Sophie passed," Adva said.

"I had a very nice cat who demanded attention."

"You must miss her. Him?"

"Him. I do. Surprising how much. I was never a cat guy."

"Where is he?" Ellen said. "Are you having him shipped here?"

Sam knew he had hesitated too long. He needed to be more aware if he was going to do what he now intended to do: kill a man, not just look him in the face. This would require far more focus, a focus he still had for writing; a focus he'd once had for loving Sophie. But nothing else. Even in football, in high school, he was second-string. He just hadn't cared enough to make it to the starting team. *Lack of focus and intensity*, his coach had admonished him. *You've got a ton of talent, son. But you just don't care enough.*

"I was going to," he said. "But then I thought it better to leave him with my next-door neighbors. They're kindhearted people. I've been fortunate like that. With nice neighbors."

"You have nice neighbors—friends—for a reason, Sam," Ellen said. "You're a nice guy."

Sam's felt light-headed. He was about to get up for some fresh air when Adva said, "Target shooting."

He forced his internal balance and stayed seated. He looked at Adva, heard her say the word "shooting" . . . wondered if he were really going mad. *Shooting. Shooting a gun at a man.*

"Target shooting. Okay—if you'll teach me, Ellen. I'll try it. It would be different."

"It'd be out of character," Adva said. "But it could be good for you. You can work some things out. It doesn't matter if it's shooting or tennis or mah-jongg. Just do one new thing."

Adva lowered her voice and leaned forward.

"I'm not saying that as a therapist, Sam, but as your friend. Okay? One new thing?"

"One new thing, Adva," Sam said.

Chapter Thirty-One

Since his banishment from Whirly's, Lee Clayborne had been eating and drinking at J's, the new Asian place next door to Whirly's, one block north, at the foot of Grove Hill. He made sure to pass by Whirly's so that whoever was behind the bar could see him walk by.

Albie, one of Johnny's bartenders, had tattoos on his neck and made it his business to look out for the women who worked there. He liked to give Lee tough-guy looks when Lee passed by. Lee didn't care about him. It was Johnny and his implacable gaze that made Lee's blood boil.

Rachel was usually there Wednesday through Saturday. Her shift began at five. She looked very fine to him, swarthy, round in the right places. Her skin looked as soft and creamy as his. She was slightly exotic, which turned him on, and rebellious toward him, which amused him. And he could tell that she was already scared.

He liked it when she didn't know he was around. When her guard was down. Twice he sat at the end of her parents' street on the cul-de-sac a few doors away from the house. Simply glancing up at her from his BlackBerry made him hard. No one questioned a late-model BMW SUV driven by a well-known developer and politician who was looking at a potential property for building ideas.

The first time Lee watched her get in her car and drive away, he waited a while and drove himself away. The next two times he watched her walk out of her house, Lee closed his eyes, stroked himself a few times, and ejaculated in his pants.

Chapter Thirty-Two

SAM'S EYES GREW ACCUSTOMED to the dim gray of the first three months of the year in Chestnut Falls.

On a late March afternoon, the sun in a cloudless sky turned the village opaque orange. He took his walk and noticed things he never had before: the window display in a new home furnishings store, the proprietor's cat in the window of a sporting goods shop. He looked in at the Christian Science Reading Room, its texts mounted on pedestals next to empty wing chairs.

He looked up and saw the second Masonic Temple built in the village—this one still in use, having replaced the original that was now the hardware store. He studied the square and compass carved in stone at the top of the third floor building façade over West Washington Street. He saw the flag flying over the decaying brick police station as it flapped eastward in the cool, blustery March breeze. He saw the varying shades of white and gray on the painted cannon that had stood on a worn brick platform on the green in front of the station since the mid-1800s, its muzzle filled with cement, no longer protecting the village from the Indians, Frenchmen, British, and Confederates who had never arrived.

He sat in the bandstand on the Village Triangle. To his left was South Franklin Street; to his right South Main. Before him, where the streets diverged at the northern tip of the Village Triangle, by the phone booth, North Main led past the Town

Hall, his office, and Whirly's, and then up Grove Hill to his house on Summit Street: the totality now of his earthly world. He admired the traditions, the architecture, yet sensed something was off. Was it him or had America begun to emanate more anger since he'd last lived in Chicago? He understood why that could be: 9/11. What he didn't know was whether the violence he felt under the surface came from the place and its people, or from him.

At a little after ten in the morning, Sam held a cardboard coffee mug from the Popcorn Shop, where he went for its view of the falls.

Instead of writing there as usual, he took his notebook and coffee across and down the street and up to his office. It was time to watch for Lee Clayborne, the man whose face he needed to see in order to somehow make sense of Sophie's death. How could he be a monster and yet fool so many in this town?

For in all his time in Chestnut Falls, Sam still had not seen him except in the newspaper, and then only twice. He found it strange how few people were out and about during the winter months—how different from Europe, where being outside was part of daily life. Still, he wondered if Lee had seen him while Sam was wandering, lost in his memories of Sophie and thoughts of vengeance. Sam could go into a zone for hours at a time and not notice a fly in his room. Sophie had loved him for his tendency to transcend, if not ignore, his surroundings. Now he wondered if he was being watched, or even followed. If so, he thought, it would be his fault for his own lack of focus.

Perhaps even more than the black-and-white photo in the newspaper, a single description from Sophie, on a drunken night when she had broken down, not long after her diagnosis, drilled itself into Sam's brain so deeply that he could not get what he imagined Lee's face to look like out of his mind. He was twenty years older now, but Sam would know him. The photo was one thing; the Lee of Sophie's nightmares, and now Sam's, another.

Back in his office, he looked out of the window at the Town Hall, where the Village Council meeting would take place that evening. At five, an hour before the roll call at council, Sam would concentrate on the building across the street.

Lee was a successful man. Sam had confirmed it from reading the local paper every day since he'd arrived. Successful men in America, Sam had heard, arrived early and stayed late.

The morning passed. He drained his cardboard coffee cup. The steam heat from the ornate, ancient silver radiator kept him warm as he wrote notes about the summer wine sent to him by his editor. Then, at a little after one o'clock, Sam took out his Swiss Army knife with the corkscrew and opened up the subject of his article, a bottle of 2007 Les Baux de Provence Rosé Domaine Mas Sainte Berthe.

As he was opening it, Jimmy Schultz knocked at his door. He held a manual Royal typewriter. Underneath was a box.

"For you."

"I don't understand." Sam opened the door all the way, nodded, and said, "Please. Enter."

"A belated welcome-to-town present. I cleaned it, replaced the rollers, put a new ribbon in it. I picked up some extra ribbons, so don't worry about that. I get a lot of stuff on eBay."

He paused, but before Sam could say anything, Jimmy continued, "All the margins work. I couldn't get the *T* to make a capital, but other than that, it's in pretty good shape. It's yours."

Sam took the machine.

"This is beautiful, Jimmy. Really beautiful."

Jimmy put the box on the floor inside Sam's office.

"I couldn't find any old-fashioned typing paper, but this will work."

He opened a package of paper. "It's regular copy paper. Maybe you can find some typing paper somewhere, you know, to keep it vintage. There's an office supply store over in Solon."

"It's really beautiful, Jimmy. This paper will be fine."

Sam ran his hand around the typewriter. It was black metal. On the left front was "Royal Portable" in ornate, gold lettering. The keys were white with black letters, indented in round metal frames. He could see all the keys, ready to strike, partly exposed, like arrows in a quiver. The spools were exposed and unused. There was nothing secretive about it, nothing that could be hacked, nothing electronic.

In Paris he had often wished he had a simple typewriter like this. He disliked the idea of the Internet, of not knowing whom he was connected to. He liked writing by hand, liked being connected to paper. But if an editor insisted, he used Sophie's computer. She'd then send his reviews and articles electronically. After she died, Sam kept her laptop but never used it, never even opened it. His editors had grudgingly come to accept the added step of transposing his longhand—usually by an intern—as his writing was legible and the word count precise.

"This is wonderful. But I can't take it. You should resell it. It's got to be worth a fair amount. It's very good of you, though."

He tapped the spacebar.

"I write by hand. My editors type my articles up. Beyond that I don't do much."

"I traded for it," Jimmy said. "I had a nineteenth-century pickax that some guy in Santa Barbara wanted for his collection. What am I going to do with an old pickax?"

He finally looked Sam directly in the eye.

"Hey, Sam. I like having a quiet renter. I like that you're a writer. It's fun for me. Slip a mention of the store in an article sometime if you want. Take the damn typewriter. I have no use for it and if I store it, it'll collect dust and end up worthless again."

Jimmy walked further into the office and placed the Royal on Sam's desk that overlooked the street and the Town Hall. He glanced down at the wine and gave Sam a smile and a nod.

"It looks good there. You've got a nice view and a new old typewriter for your work. You're all set."

"Thanks, Jimmy. *Merci beaucoup.*"

Jimmy smiled. Sam forced a smile and patted the typewriter. After all these years of longhand, Sam felt a touch of excitement looking at it. His hand was tired from writing. He was tired. Maybe this would help him write as he waited for his chance to confront Clayborne.

Jimmy walked down the steep, shallow stairs, then outside and back into the hardware store.

Sam sat down at his desk and took his first sip of wine. He tasted and identified all of the five grapes that made up the blend: grenache, syrah, mourvedre, cinsault, and cabernet sauvignon. He closed his eyes and thought of the wild strawberries that grew along the path to the sea outside the cottage in Ville de Rachat.

There he would drink a wine like this and think only of Sophie. There, too, his senses would be filled with the smell of strawberries and lavender and sunflowers, of pastures and vineyards and the sea, but mostly of the earth that had held him there and had kept him alive.

He tore off a piece of the sourdough bread he'd bought a day earlier at a new bakery that had opened at the south end of town. It had gone stale, but he was hungry and ate the rest of the loaf and drank half the bottle of rosé.

Today the light was too similar to the south of France. It was in Ville de Rachat, more than in Paris, where he imagined her, even though she had never been there when she was alive. Yet he could even now feel his thoughts of Sophie being replaced. Now, it was Lee Clayborne, a man he'd never met, whom he hated as much as he loved Sophie, who would not leave his mind and soul alone.

Chapter Thirty-Three

THE LAST DAY OF March was sunny and cool. Ellen, having been frustrated earlier in the day in her attempt to find Sam at home, walked down Grove Hill from her studio and headed toward the hardware store.

She and Adva had argued the night before, and now she replayed their words in her head.

"Why are so intent on bring this emotionally crippled man back into the world?" Ellen had asked. "Why can't we leave him alone and enjoy his company when he pokes his head out? Why drag him back to a world he wants to escape?"

"He needs help," Adva said.

"Maybe he needs solitude, Adva. Not everyone has to fit some pattern of mental health that fits into one of your categories. Everyone, one way or another, writes their own story. They wrap it in the covers of their own books. Some want others to read their book. Others want to keep their bloodstained pages to themselves. Adva, for God's sake, what don't you get? Sam wants to keep his to himself. What's wrong with that? Why don't you just let him be?"

"You know what, Ellen? You really piss me off. Sam's a decent guy whose wife died. What don't *you* get about that? You've lost people—you dad, your mom, friends . . . right? He's just trying to heal. Just like you had to heal. Just like I did."

Ellen stood, grim-faced, blood rising to her head.

"For whatever reason, Ellen, he's comfortable with you," Adva said. "That's easy to see."

"Really? I see it differently. I see a guy who can't admit to himself he's attracted to you—and a woman who can't admit he's attracted to her."

Oh, shit, Ellen thought. *I did it.*

Adva said nothing for some long moments. Her brown eyes were lost behind tears.

Finally, her voice shaking, she said, "I've seen this kind of fragility before in people and it doesn't *fucking end well*, Ellen. How *dare* you? This isn't about attraction. This is about a guy whose grief is making him drift into a netherworld where ending one's life simply becomes rational. This guy may be headed for one of these days becoming his *last* day. Ellen, he's in trouble. Can't you see he's in trouble?"

Ellen moved toward Adva and put her arms around her.

"I'm sorry," she said. "I'm really sorry. This is my fault."

She had said that, but today she still believed Adva and Sam shared something she didn't understand. Something like attraction, but not quite. What lay between attraction and repulsion? Friendship? Something deeper and unspoken. Ellen sensed that neither Adva nor Sam knew what it was, and that made their friendship nearly unbearable for Ellen, who felt she was in a play where the other actors were invisible.

Ellen continued down Grove Hill and walked into the hardware store.

"Where Sam's office?" Ellen demanded of Jimmy Schultz, who was arranging a window display. "I know you're hiding him here." She forced a laugh.

Ellen bought as many supplies as possible from the hardware store. What she couldn't buy there, he ordered for her, more as a favor than anything else. But while she considered Jimmy

Schultz a friend, she knew Jimmy didn't give away personal information without a reason. He couldn't give her what she wanted: to know why Sam was in town.

"You know Sam?" Jimmy said.

"He's our neighbor, and a friend. He told us about his new office. He is here, right? Which office? There's no sign outside the building. That figures, knowing him."

She stared at the ceiling, as if trying to see through to the second floor.

Jimmy looked at Ellen over his reading glasses and sighed.

"Don't burn me on this. I have a code," he said, not unpleasantly.

"You're pissing me off, James," Ellen said.

"Promise me."

Ellen took a deep breath and said, "If I'm ever on the run, remind me to have you hide me out."

"You don't even want to know the nooks and crannies of this building. Lots of secret places. The Masons continue to surprise me. Remind me to show you the third floor sometime." Jimmy paused and squinted at Ellen. "All right. Go out the front door; it's the next door on the right, up the stairs, first office on the right."

Ellen turned toward the door. "Thanks," she said. "And don't worry; I'm not a stalker."

"Wait. Any chance you can call him first?"

Ellen turned to Jimmy. She folded her arms.

"He doesn't have a cell phone. He doesn't have the Internet. He doesn't have a landline. Jimmy, don't you find that odd?"

"None of my business," Jimmy said.

"Not even a little strange?"

Jimmy took off his reading glasses, sat sideways on the counter, and looked at Ellen.

"Half of us would love to live that way. Don't you think?" he said.

Ellen softened, sat next to him.

"I suppose," she said. "Still."

"I thought you were friends with him."

"We are, but it just really struck me. It doesn't feel quite right. I worry. We worry."

"You seem steamed today," Jimmy said. "Everything okay on the home front?"

"Ask Adva."

"Hey," Jimmy said. "Come on. You two are my last best hope to be part of a happy couple that actually stays together."

"Forget I said that. All right?" Ellen said. "We all have our bad days."

Jimmy began walking to the paint room.

"Remember," he said, disappearing around the corner. "I have a code."

Chapter Thirty-Four

ON FRIDAY, THE DAY before Sam was to go with Ellen to the target range, he left his article on a Domaine des Perdrix Burgundy unfinished, like his half-filled wineglass, to go for a walk.

He'd been transported by the wine's nose, complexity, and finish and he wanted to mix it with fresh air. The steam heat of his office was no way to take in this Burgundy and properly write about it. A fireplace or woodstove might do, but he didn't want to return to his desolate house and go through the trouble of building a fire.

Spring-fevered schoolchildren filled the late-afternoon streets. Sam, in his watch cap, gloves, and parka, couldn't understand the way they dressed. The air was damp, the temperature in the low forties, yet most wore hoodies as their only protection from the weather. Some were in T-shirts, and a tall, skinny boy wore long madras shorts and flip-flops. Sam wondered if living here had somehow thickened their blood, or if it was just youth. On this early April day, he was chilled to his bones.

Was this the way Sophie had been before he'd met her? He imagined her like this, ignoring the chill, or the heat, or the rain, the fog or the smog of California when she was growing up.

"I loved my childhood," she'd told him in Paris one evening. "Isn't that different and funny? Don't most people regret their childhood in some way? I didn't, not at all," Sophie had said, answering her own question, a trait he had adored. "Did you, Sam? Did you love your childhood? You didn't, did you? You probably brooded, even in junior high school. Oh, I wish I'd known you then. I could have brought you out of it."

Sam remembered this conversation in the chilly Ohio spring air. He had loved the aching chill of Paris. Now when he thought of Sophie he also thought of her joy and Lee Clayborne's brutality, turning, turning in Sam's mind even as he walked down the cheerful street. Raping Sophie, who begged him to stop. And during and afterward pounding, pounding, pounding her head against the floor and the wall. He thought, *For so long that she could have died at any time. Lee wanted to kill her.*

Sam stopped at the bridge and looked over it. It wasn't a terribly long drop to the falls, perhaps thirty feet, but the rocks were jagged and sharp, and there was moss that must grow year round, slippery moss that would take him over and down to the jagged rock. He looked over, grasped at the cold green railing, grasped it and clenched and hated so deeply that he could not take this way out and end his own life. He needed to end another's first.

He walked into the warmth of the Hearthside Bookshop, past the falls and across from the Village Triangle. At the front of the store were the staff picks and new titles. He read paragraphs from a few new books, but nothing grabbed him. He turned and walked across the room to the nonfiction section and picked up a coffee table book on gardening. He wanted to know what the foliage would look like should his mission take him through the summer.

As he looked at the photos, he imagined living here with Sophie. Yes, she would have changed his childhood. He'd had a reasonably happy one, but with her, or had he met her in high school or college, who knows how life could have changed for both of them? So many regrets over things he could never change.

With each photo more lush and vibrant than the last, his anger grew at what she—and they—would miss. It was more verdant here than in the south of France, if not as colorful; as well, the gardens seemed wilder than the ornate, sculpted gardens of Paris with the exception of le parc Monceau. Mostly he saw photos of deep green foliage and wildflowers, if only for a few months a year. He suddenly understood the term "the New World," with its tangle of lush charms and coarse discomforts.

They could have had a new world, one of their own, if only things had been different in Sophie's past, if only there had been no night of horror with Lee Clayborne, if only her trauma had not simmered in her brain, unable to find a physical and psychological escape route, boiling into the tumor that cut short her life and their love while they were young.

Had they discovered this place on a random drive from Chicago to New York on holiday, maybe they would have stayed. They would have lived quietly. They could again be Americans, this time together.

The page of the gardening book blurred until the photo become Impressionist. Sam thought how Sophie would have liked Ellen and Adva and Michael Shield and Johnny Kenston and Jimmy Schultz. Sophie would have spent hours at the hardware store browsing the knickknacks. There were two wine distributors within ten miles of Chestnut Falls—she could have easily found work here. They could have loved each other here.

They could have loved each other anywhere.

Sam was deep inside a photo of a cottage garden when he felt someone standing to his left.

First he saw the hands, holding a book, attached to a man with manicured fingernails. The hands were medium-sized, but strong. Around his right wrist was a watch with a black alligator wristband and Roman numerals on the face. Sam knew the watch, had seen advertisements for it in the expensive magazines that ran his articles. This was not a watch for merely telling time.

Sam froze. He had never considered himself psychic, or prescient, or even particularly instinctive, yet he knew those hands, and to whom they were connected.

How did he know this? The way a dog knows his master is five miles away and driving home. The way one spouse knows the other has cheated. The only way anyone really knows anything without evidence.

He stopped breathing. The hands turned a page. The book was a biography of Churchill.

Sam made himself breathe. He looked straight ahead.

The man attached to the manicured hands was motionless. Sam did not look at the man and sensed he was reading intently. Those hands—the manicure fit but didn't fit. Those hands, as if disconnected from a body, seemed like shining lethal weapons, capable of grabbing Sophie by the neck, slamming her to the ground, slapping her, raping her, smashing her head . . .

Sam's legs began to shake. He steadied himself. He forced himself to look to his left. The man whose manicured, lethal hands held the book looked to his right.

Sam's eyes looked into the other man's eyes. An overhead halogen light reflected into the man's blue eyes; in the man's eyes, Sam saw his own face looking back at him.

The man nodded at Sam and smiled. He then nodded down to Sam's book and said, "Won't be long. The gardens will be in bloom and all will again be right with the world."

Then he went back to reading his book on Churchill. Sam

stared at his own book, the Impressionist blur. Soon the man slapped his book shut and turned toward the man at the counter.

"You made a sale, Phil. Ring up the Churchill bio. I'll pay cash."

The man tucked the book under his arm and turned back toward Sam. He put out his right hand, his perfect, gleaming fingernails a contrast to Sam's nails, cut slightly jagged with the scissors on his army knife, and his fingers, which were slimmer, longer, and Sam, realized, weaker.

"Lee Clayborne," the man said. "I've seen you around a few times. You're the writer, right? Welcome. Let me know if this town gets to you—it can be a tad stodgy."

Sam took his hand and shook it.

"If you get spring fever we'll tip a few back. New place just opened up down the street. I'd avoid Whirly's, if you haven't already. The owner's a psycho. It's not his fault. PTSD from Vietnam. Tough break. But he's too unpredictable for a town like ours. We take care of our own here."

His toxic mixture of chilling charisma and violent magnetism nearly dropped Sam to the floor. And it was over before Sam realized that he'd taken Lee's business card with his office phone number on it. Sam took it out of instinct because that's what normal men did—accept a handshake and business card.

With a smile born out of his desire to kill Lee Clayborne, Sam said: "I look forward to getting together."

Chapter Thirty-Five

MINUTES LATER, SAM WALKED into Whirly's and ordered a whiskey. Rachel asked him what kind and he remembered that here it didn't automatically mean Scotch, so he said, "Scotch." She asked him what kind of Scotch and he said, "Pick one, please."

She poured him a Dewar's neat. He drank it quickly. Whiskey had been his drink of choice in his twenties. He rarely drank more than one glass of hard liquor, except at Adva and Ellen's. Too much made him agitated and aggressive. Tonight he needed quick obliteration.

Rachel was the only server at Whirly's. Sam sensed she wanted to be friendly but he had nothing to say. They'd only exchanged pleasantries before. There was something about this young woman that reminded him of Sophie. It wasn't physical—even their voices were completely different: Sophie's had been low but vibrant, Rachel's was choppier, with a Midwestern flatness. But there was something.

Now that he had seen Clayborne, everyone and everything in this town that had charmed him for a few months was stained with blood, corroded with evil.

Late afternoon turned into night. As he drank, Sam's French-inflected thinking emerged; the consistent English that had so easily returned to him disappeared as his thoughts became jumbled. French and English mixed. Places mixed. The French he'd assimilated while in France was stronger in his mind than he'd realized.

"*Je suis ici, pas là.*"

"I am here," he reminded himself. "Not there."

"*Tu connais Lee Clayborne?*"

"I'm not sure what you're saying."

"Do you know Lee Clayborne?"

Hours had passed and Sam was on his sixth Scotch. Rachel dreaded cutting him off. He hadn't bothered anyone. Where was Johnny? He normally never left on a Friday night, but his aunt was ill and he had to sit with her until his uncle returned home.

When had Johnny said his uncle's second shift ended? Eleven? It was nearing midnight. Rachel hated being alone in the bar.

A group from Gates Mills came in. Rachel had noticed before that the very rich rarely caused the trouble that the merely rich ones like Lee caused. There were about ten of them. Five couples. Voices full of money, always, but the air around them was full of it too: the wafting smells of leather and expensive perfume and faint traces of where they'd been earlier, one of the best restaurants in downtown Cleveland. She felt their wealth and security: the serene joy of having, the peace of not owing.

She had learned, growing up around them, and working here at Whirly's, that the very rich had more moments of joy than others, despite the claims of self-help literature meant to soothe and tempt the lower and middle and upper-middle classes and take a small piece of their wallets. Rachel saw it night after night: with rare exception, usually because of drugs or illness, the very rich did feel better about themselves.

Tonight she needed their combined billion-dollar confidence. She turned again to Sam. She liked him. He seemed smart and kind but very sad. He was too old for her, too beaten up, but a younger version of him, perhaps . . .

What possible connection could he have with Lee Clayborne?

"Yes, Sam. I know him."

"You know my name?"

"We've talked, Sam. A few times."

Sam shook his head back and forth.

"*Je suis très ivre.*"

While she tried to listen to Sam, Rachel took orders from the Gates Mills customers. A man in a blue blazer and open-necked, pink oxford shirt with cufflinks was ordering. He stopped and smiled, nodded toward Sam.

"I can wait," he said. "Your friend is telling you he's drunk."

He knitted his eyebrows and gave her a closed-mouth smile that said: *I understand. And I speak French for all the right reasons.*

"Sam, please, one moment," Rachel said.

Who are these people? Sam wondered. *Are they his people?*

She filled the orders for the Gates Mills group. Two of the women in the group thanked her. One complimented her on her hair, another on her blouse. One of them called her "honey" and said to her friends, "She's adorable. She reminds me of my Emily."

The room was spinning. Sam felt sick. He willed his stomach to calm down enough to keep him from vomiting. Rachel turned to him after ten minutes of filling the group's drinks and food orders. Pâté and salmon, fruit and cheese now mixed with their other scents, and the group was, for a few moments, sated.

"*Je suis très ivre.*"

"That gentleman says you're saying you're drunk. Is that right?" Rachel said to Sam. "Is that what you're saying? I don't speak French."

"Lee Clayborne," Sam said.

Panic rose through her stomach into her throat. Where was Johnny?

Sam looked up at Rachel.

"*Tu le connais?* You know him?"

He looked in her frightened eyes.

"You know him," he said.

The pink-shirted man said, "I'm sorry," and looked at Sam and put his hand on his forearm. He hadn't heard Sam and Rachel's conversation.

"Just one sec, I'll be one sec . . . Rachel, is it? Could we have a couple more pomegranate martinis? For the couple that just joined us."

He smiled and tossed her two twenties.

"Let me pay for these now."

He smiled again, called to the new couple, "You have to try these."

"Change?" Rachel held up the money.

The pink-shirted man looked back at her. He was hugging the female in the couple.

"No, no . . . I keep interrupting," he said. "You keep it." He smiled, winked, put his other arm around the male.

Rachel took one of the twenties and put her 100 percent tip in the jar by the cash register. She turned again to Sam.

"I'm sorry, Sam, it's a difficult time to talk."

Sam threw down his own money for his drinks. He grabbed his coat and lunged out the door, slipped down the stone steps, nearly fell. He bumped into a couple as he stumbled across the stone patio, out onto River Street.

It was Tom, one of Lee's friends, who had started coming back to Whirly's the day after St. Patrick's Day. Sam staggered near him and Tom gave him a shoulder shove. Sam fell into the street.

"Watch it, asshole," Tom said.

Sam tried to stand, slipped, and fell on his face, rolled over, stood up, fell again, humiliated.

He ignored Tom. "I'm sorry," he called out to Rachel, into the cold night air, though she couldn't hear him through the window and the din in the bar. "I'm sorry." He didn't exactly know for what, but he needed to say it to someone.

Sam walked unsteadily, tried to light a cigarette halfway up Grove Hill. He shook too badly to get the match to the tip of the cigarette. He felt rage exploding up through him, grabbed the cigarette package out of his parka's pocket, crumpled it, and threw it to the ground. He stomped the cigarette package into the sidewalk.

Under the cold, clear, starry Chestnut Falls night, a half block from his house, Sam Koppang looked up. The sky was clear and there was a full moon, full of sadness, full of the loss of Sophie to the world below it, full of the tragedy that had brought him to this village where he had become a liar to the people who cared about him and a fool to those who did not.

Chapter Thirty-Six

SAM OPENED HIS EYES at a quarter past 11:00 a.m. The sun poured in through the south window. Ellen sat in his guest chair, reading the Saturday paper.

There was a fire in the woodstove, and it was warm in the kitchen. Sam was on the floor, a blanket over him and a pillow beneath his head. A new coffeemaker sat on the counter.

Earlier that morning, Ellen had banged on the door and seen Sam lying there. She tried the back door. It was open, and she went inside. At first, seeing him crumpled on the floor, she thought he could be dead. After checking for signs of life and determining that he was alive but hung over, she took her cell phone out of the back pocket of her jeans.

"James, I'm not going to make target practice . . ."

She left the house and went to CVS and bought a coffeemaker, a bottle of aspirin, and a newspaper. She bought bagels and a pound of coffee from Einstein's. Then she came back, made the coffee, sat in his guest chair, ate a bagel, read the *Times,* and waited for two and a half hours. The sun warmed her back and relaxed her.

The coffeemaker was black and basic with an on/off button. There was a full carafe of coffee already brewed, and there were bagels with an unopened package of cream cheese. Sam's house was more of a home now than it had been since he'd moved in.

As he woke, Sam smelled the coffee. He didn't remember getting home. He didn't remember much. He didn't want to. Not yet.

He shielded his eyes from the sun and squinted into Ellen's. "Coffee?" she said.

"Water first? I can get it."

Sam started to get up, felt light-headed, and lay back down. Ellen took one of Sam's few glasses and filled it with tap water, then leaned down and gave it to Sam along with three aspirin. Ellen filled it up again and he drank another glass.

"Coffee now would be wonderful."

He took the mug of black coffee from her and drank a little and said, "Oh, *merde*. Target practice."

"Yes, at eight a.m. I'm afraid we're late."

"Can we still go?"

"No big deal. I called my friends at my club and told them my guest was shit-faced and passed out on his floor. You smell like a distillery, by the way. Single malt?"

"No. Dewar's. Lots."

"Ah, yes. Dewar's. Goes down like water after the first few," she said.

"Comes up like fire," Sam said. "My throat is raw."

Sam drank some coffee, gulped painfully, and sat up, still on the floor, his back against the wall, taking in the heat from Ellen's fire.

"Nice," he said.

"It should be. It's my dry kindling. I have a stash you don't know about."

"I'll be sure to pinch some when I find it."

"I'm sure you will."

She poured herself a mug of coffee.

"I suggest you stay put for a while. You have that look of

potential throwing up about you. Which I suppose would do you good. But I don't want to clean up, so just sit there. Bagel?"

"I can try."

Ellen split a bagel and put some cream cheese on it. She got a small plate from the cupboard, inspected it, rinsed it, dried it with a paper towel, and handed it to Sam.

"Eat slowly."

"I didn't eat yesterday."

"You don't say. I never would have guessed."

Sam took a bite. He chewed slowly. He looked up at Ellen's face, at her creases, her smooth salt-and-pepper hair, her dark brown Chippewa eyes.

He let out a long sigh. The fire and blanket were warm. The coffee and bagel tasted good.

After a few moments he said:

"If I ever loved again. Not that I will. But if I ever did, I would fall in love with—"

"Adva."

"I was going to say you," Sam said.

"I know. And you'd be wrong. I think that's what in Adva's business they call 'transference.' You trust me. You'd love her. If you don't already."

"I don't already."

"Well, take your time on that answer. Anyway, you're still drunk. That's sort of fun."

"Where is she, by the way?" Sam said.

"Clients on Saturdays."

"Oh. Right. Hence your target shooting."

"And whatever else I can do to occupy my Saturdays until she gets home."

They sat in silence for a while. Ellen slid down off her chair and sat next to Sam.

"I love her very much, Sam."

They stared into the fire.

"I know. And she loves you very much. That's obvious."

"Yes, I suppose she does. Maybe she does."

"What does that mean?"

"It means I'm fourteen years older than Adva. She was in a heterosexual marriage. I'm insecure. Shall I continue?"

Ellen put her head on Sam's shoulder. He put his arm around her. She was large-boned and well muscled and it felt awkward but nice to have his arm around her. It had been about five years since he'd had his arm around a woman.

"But I do love you as a friend," he said.

"The feeling is almost mutual," Ellen said.

Sam took another bite of the bagel.

"Almost?"

"I like you as a friend. For me to love you as a friend you have to be honest."

Both of them took a sip of coffee.

"I should warm these up. And stoke the fire," Ellen said.

"Okay."

She poured fresh coffee and threw on more kindling. She sat back down and put her head on his shoulder.

"For goodness sakes, put your damn arm back around me. Friend."

He did. Then he said, "Honest with you."

Ellen turned to look at Sam.

"Yes. Honest with me."

"About."

"About why you're here. About what's going on with you. I mean, come on."

"To write. Did I ever tell you how I picked Chestnut Falls?"

"That story about how your editor's assistant lived here and talked about it once, and you didn't want to go to New York or San Francisco, and you were in a brandy haze, and you were sick of France? That story?"

"Yes," he said.

"That's why I don't love you as a friend."

"Why?"

Ellen let out a long sigh and gently took his hand and removed his arm from her shoulder. "Because that story is a lie. Right, Sam?"

Sam didn't answer.

"Look, Sam. Adva loves you—on some level, at least—because you bring out something in her. You make her feel . . . I don't know . . . like a part of her is still vital. The hetero part, maybe. Not that she'd admit it, but I can see it. It's nobody's fault. We're all made the way we're made. And it's something I have to learn to live with, whether it comes out around you or some other guy. She's bisexual, or thinks she is. Whatever that means. But whatever it means, I'm not it."

Sam remained silent.

"I only know that being bisexual isn't about just sex," she said. "It's about the ability to romantically love someone. She thinks she can't be in love with you romantically, at least not yet. So she can love you as a friend. Because . . ."

She took a sip of coffee.

"Because?" Sam said.

"Because she's willing to overlook the big lie. That's where the romance comes in."

Sam was quiet; he knew what was coming.

"The big lie about why you came to this village, Sam."

Again Ellen turned to Sam.

"I can't ignore that or love you as a friend. I'm a simple person. I sculpt. I walk my dog. I love my partner. I have a few hobbies from childhood. The shooting, the archery, chopping wood. I do things with my hands. I need to keep my mind clear and simple. I can't abide lies, Sam. Little ones, from Adva, maybe, because I love her romantically. But not from a friend. Not a big whopper from a friend."

The fire crackled and the last of the March ice fell in slushy chunks from the roof and hit the back deck as it warmed up outside.

"What can I say, Ellen?" Sam said.

"You'll admit the story about the brandy fog is a lie?"

"Yes."

"Will you tell me why you're here?"

Sam said nothing. He drank some coffee.

She took another deep breath.

"I don't think you have any intention of telling me, but I still want to know. If and when you're ready, you tell me. In return, I'm going to make you a promise. If you tell me, if you relieve yourself of whatever awful burden you're carrying, I will hold your secret. No matter what it is."

Ellen stood up and looked down at Sam.

"Did you hear that?"

"Yes."

"When you're ready?"

"Yes."

"For sure, Sam? Can you promise?"

Sam's head was throbbing, but he felt relaxed. He wanted to stay in front of this fire all day. He was tired, wanted to sleep again.

"Sam? Can you promise that, at least?"

He looked up at Ellen, his friend, whether he wanted a friend or not. He wanted badly to tell her yes. Yet he could not abide telling another lie to her, not sitting here with one of the only people he cared about, one of the only people who cared about him.

"No. I can't tell you, Ellen."

"Dammit, Sam. I mean, really. That hurts me. Do you understand why?"

"Of course."

"So you don't trust me."

"I trust you."

"Then tell me what's going on. Who moves here, alone, from France, rents a little office over the hardware store, has no phone, doesn't use a computer? This is insane. I'd ask if you were a spy if you weren't such a bumbling idiot sometimes. Sam, you couldn't spy on yourself. So what are you?"

"Listen," Sam said. "Last night I acted crazy, but I'm not crazy. I know how I must look to you, to Adva, to the people at that bar, maybe even to Mike."

"Then tell me what's going on. Sam. *Tell me what's going on.*"

"No. I can't. I can't tell you, Ellen. I'm sick from not being able to. But I cannot, I absolutely cannot."

Sam looked into the fire and Ellen looked at Sam. "What a waste," she said.

He looked at her, shocked. "What? Why?"

"Figure it out," Ellen said as she stood up. She looked down at him.

"I'm sorry. I'm very sorry, Ellen."

Ellen walked across the room, washed out her cup, and turned to look at Sam, who was still huddled under the blanket.

"So am I," she said. "Very." Then she left quietly out the back door.

For the rest of the day, Sam barely moved except to throw logs in the woodstove. He knew the time to act was coming, but he wanted one more meeting with Lee Clayborne first.

Chapter Thirty-Seven

APRIL 9. 4:00 A.M., an hour when nearly everyone in Chestnut Falls was asleep, the exceptions being a couple of cops on patrol, Anita the police dispatcher, a clerk at the all-night BP gas station, a few depressed web surfers, the *Plain Dealer* delivery man, some late-night drinkers, some insomniacs, a few first-shift workers, and some methamphetamine addicts. And Lee Clayborne.

Lee's business was in the toilet. He saw no way out without Father's help, yet again, and that was only slightly better than the alternative, which was bankruptcy. At least after bankruptcy he could still tap his trust fund, leave town, and teach skiing in Vail, which is all he'd ever really wanted to do anyway. That was still a possibility, if this bailout didn't do the trick.

He'd built eight houses on spec, with the idea of making Clayborne Homes the hottest brand in the Valley's premium market. Now the housing market was in the worst dive in memory, with no end in sight.

How could he have known what would happen? For ten years he'd sold half-million- to two-million-dollar houses easily. Moving from real estate sales to being a developer was a no-brainer. But the banks started failing—his father had predicted it—and money got tight. When a Clayborne couldn't get a bank loan, the world was going to hell.

He needed money, but not one or two hundred thousand

dollars like the other times. Now a half million would barely cover his losses and keep him solvent, and even then he'd need to sell a couple of spec houses quickly. He had no choice but to accept his father's offer. Yet that would mean another kind of defeat. It was bad enough his father knew how he'd screwed up on his spec houses. Worse yet would be accepting the money that Father used as a weapon the way he'd once used his perverted sexuality. His prick and his power, that's what his father knew about. But if he didn't take it, the bottom would drop out and Lee Clayborne would be the laughingstock of the Chestnut Valley.

Lee had stopped calling Rachel, but he could not stop thinking about her, so he fantasized, and planned.

She was different: pretty and clearly smart. She made Lee think of Sophie, his college sweetheart. Sophie, confident and beautiful. Lying there he wondered: what if he hadn't lost his temper with her that night? They would have made a beautiful couple, made beautiful babies. He wouldn't be a bachelor approaching forty years old. Seldom did Lee Clayborne question his past, yet tonight he wondered whether he had destroyed his one good chance at love. Sophie had had it all.

There had been others after her, plenty of them, and the ones that he didn't dump got the hint and disappeared on their own. Only three had been special enough for him to pursue. Sophie was the first.

Then, foolishly, and against his mother's advice, Lee hooked up with Adva and let himself fall for her hot doctor routine. He knew he didn't love her when he saw her walk down the aisle. After a couple years of treating her like a princess, playing house, he got fully sick of her intellectual bullshit, of her questioning him when he showed up hammered or late for dinner, or didn't show up at all. She'd turned into a cloying brown bitch.

Rachel reminded him of Sophie. She was ambitious, attractive, innocent, and she needed someone to protect her. So she was young, so what? So he'd gotten drunk at Whirly's, so what? All Kenston had to do was let him pay his check and leave. Instead Johnny Kenston banished *him*? Humiliated *him* in front of a young woman who embodied what he'd lost? Fuck Johnny Kenston. He was a self-righteous asshole. Lee knew all about Johnny in Vietnam, shooting up a village in Vietnam. The fucker didn't even deserve to live, much less throw him out of a bar and make an ass out of him in front of Rachel Rosen.

He'd ruin Kenston, who would never even know how it happened. Lee had friends on the police department, on the zoning commission, in the health inspector's office. Power had its perks.

His teeth-grinding fury at Johnny, his need to get back at him stirred Lee and turned to sexual desire for Rachel in a split second. Lee had applied his No Penetration rule to most of the other women he'd been with over the years since high school, but now he couldn't imagine withholding from Rachel. Penetration was a reward he gave to special women. He could live without intercourse, which, for Lee, led to nothing good. It really was for them, a show of generosity. It was not the way he preferred his sex.

At 4:30 a.m. Lee, his body wrung out from hours of working out earlier, and tired of Johnny Kenston inhabiting his thoughts, fantasized about Rachel. He thought mostly of the V of her neckline. Her skin looked smooth and Mediterranean. He stroked his own skin and imagined that hers was even smoother.

He completed his fantasy, but it relieved nothing except, momentarily, his physical urges. Rachel resided now only in his mind. She was there to stay.

Planning was everything. And so he decided: he would gladly take this bailout from Father, and with that, Lee would give himself one more chance to really break through, to run with the big dogs in Greater Cleveland, to get in on the serious development projects, the ones with eight and nine figures attached to them. The deals that would make his parents—and everyone else—realize what he was really made of.

More important, he realized that the bailout was a sign that he had one more chance to find the woman of his destiny and do it right this time. No more overly sensitive *artistes* like Sophie, who disappeared on him. No more latent lesbians like Adva. He wanted a nice, simple girl, one who would appreciate what he had to offer. He wanted Rachel.

As Lee Clayborne finally drifted off to sleep, he was comforted in the knowledge that he had found the right woman at last. When the bailout came through in the next few weeks, he would celebrate with Rachel.

As sleep began to overtake him, he could think of a real future, a normal future, one with Rachel.

Something jolted him upright and his heart beat faster than during a workout—an unfamiliar feeling to him, this anxiety from a mere thought. Where *had* Sophie gone? Then he remembered a conversation with a fraternity brother who had e-mailed him years ago about a wild trip he'd taken. The fraternity brother had seen Sophie. Where was it? Lee hadn't given it much thought. He was on to other things. A city. New York? He took a deep breath and tried to remember.

His fraternity brother—who'd never had a clue about what Lee had done to Sophie that night, no one had—had seen Sophie in a café as he was walking down a street. Sophie looked older, he'd told Lee, but unmistakably and beautifully Sophie. She was laughing, touching a man's face, drinking wine. The fraternity brother had gone in to say hello. Sophie had seemed startled, even a little frightened. Still, they had talked, and the brother had learned that Sophie was married. She and her husband—the man she was with—lived in Paris. The brother did not bring up Lee's name—Lee had told him they'd had a bad falling out, that's all. Sophie seemed happy with her husband. Then Lee remembered one more thing his fraternity brother had told him. That her husband was also from the States. And that his occupation was something Lee's fraternity brother found humorous: Sophie's husband made his living writing about wine.

Chapter Thirty-Eight

A WEEK AFTER THEIR CHANCE meeting at the bookstore, Sam made a call from the phone booth on the Village Triangle and asked Lee Clayborne to meet him for a drink. Lee agreed.

"Give me a half hour," Lee said. "Meet me at J's."

Sam walked through town for a while, then to J's.

The place was packed. In the third weekend of April, the temperature had climbed to the sixties. Tax returns were finished. Mating season had begun in The Bubble, and partyers who weren't in the central village were at one of the three restaurant-bars that formed a cluster just west of J's and Whirly's—Hunter's Tavern, Alec's Café, and Tommy's Bistro.

He avoided the outdoor patio where the smokers hung out. After tossing his pack of cigarettes on the street that drunken night, Sam hadn't bought any more.

Sam thought of a Buddhist teaching Sophie had told him about: Shed your bad habits so you don't take them with you to the next life.

The two men met inside J's and shook hands. This time Sam was prepared. Lee's handshake was just right. Not too hard and not too weak, it was the handshake of a man who had been taught well by his father.

Sam matched his handshake grip for grip.

"Good to see you," Lee said.

"You, too. How was the Churchill book?"

"What Churchill book?" Lee asked.

They walked to a corner booth and sat down. Lee faced the room.

Rather than forcing his eyes to hold Lee's gaze, Sam acted distracted. He figured that people expected laser focus from salesmen and surgeons, not from writers.

"Nice place. I haven't been here," Sam said, looking around. His back to the room, he had the excuse to look over his shoulder as he composed himself.

"The book," he repeated, gazing at the tin-plate ceiling. "It was good?"

Lee yawned. He paused just long enough to let Sam know he was indulging his small talk.

"Oh, right. The Churchill book. I'm a biography buff. Can't get enough of them, especially ones about great men from the mother country. Hold on."

A server, Carrie, came to their table.

"Sam? Wine, beer, cocktail?" Lee said. "Darlene behind the bar makes a killer martini, if you like your drinks old school. Gin, of course. Leave the vodka to the ladies."

"And James Bond. He drank vodka martinis," Sam replied, thinking, *You philistine punk,* but quickly calmed himself. *Don't let him bait you,* he thought. "Beer's fine. Whatever you suggest on tap. It's your neck of the woods, Lee."

"Try the Great Lakes. Good local brew."

"Sounds fine," Sam said and nodded to Carrie.

"I said it was good. Not fine. Anyway, Bombay Sapphire up, dry, two olives, Carrie," Lee said. "Thanks."

Sam jumped in. "Tell me about yourself, Lee. We didn't get much of a chance to talk last week."

"Boring. But okay. Mayflower and founding father ancestors, mother's D.A.R., too, blah blah, you get the idea. Nothing special."

Sam now felt as if his blood were flowing through a frozen pipe.

Lee waved to a couple who had come in the door, nodded to several other patrons.

"You're a popular guy," Sam said. "Seems like everybody knows you."

Lee leaned back in the retro-fifties booth.

"Oh, they usually want something. Of course it's a myth that I can do anything for them. I'm a small-town councilman. I can't really do much for anyone."

Sam took in Lee's pitch-perfect false modesty. He knew from working the city desk at the *Tribune* that local politics could make and break those who played them well, or poorly.

For the first time in his life, Sam wished he had a gun. Then he remembered what Erasmo had said: "*Tu as l'air d'un homme qui a de la haine dans son coeur.* You have the look of one with hatred in his heart."

Yes, he hated. Erasmo had been right. He hated and he didn't care anymore.

"All politics is local. Isn't that the expression?" Sam said "I seem to remember that from when I was younger. Who said that?"

"Tip O'Neill," Lee said. "Good memory."

"Democrat, right? Boston?" Sam said. "I'm guessing you're the Grand Old Party? This seems like a pretty conservative place."

"I'm an independent," Lee said, obviously annoyed. "Only way to go. I vote for the best woman. Or man. I'm surprised you resort to cheap stereotypes. Being a *Frenchman* and all."

The beer and cocktail came. They toasted.

"Here's to being independent," Sam said.

"Hear, hear," Lee said. "Don't tread on me."

"You got that right," Sam said.

"You've spent a lot of time in France, right?"

Sam knew the implication. "Most of my adult life. But, look. The French get a bad rap. Some of the toughest men you'll ever meet are French special forces."

"I'm sure they are," Lee said. "The French are wonderful allies. They've really been there for us, haven't they?"

Sam ignored the sarcasm, knew he was being baited again and ignored it. They took a drink. Sam looked around.

"Some nice-looking ladies," Sam said. He sounded alien to himself.

"Absolutely. It's no Paris, but it's not too shabby. And these ladies shave their legs. And armpits."

"Not too shabby at all," Sam said. *Control*, he said to himself. *Control*.

Sam leaned back, put his right arm on the top of his side of the booth. He felt his heart hammering inside.

"You seem like a guy who would've gotten caught by now. No?"

"Caught?" Lee's mouth twisted and he raised his eyes. "What does that mean?"

"You with anyone? That's all."

"Oh," Lee said. "You're asking me the 'You're almost forty and never been married' question. No, I'm not gay. Not that there's anything wrong with that."

"I'm sorry?" Sam said.

"An old line from a TV show. *Seinfeld*? No? You never saw it?"

He tried to look puzzled and pleasant. Closed-mouth smile.

"I've been out of the loop, as they say."

"On the moon? Anyway, seriously, I was married once. I try to avoid the subject."

"Local gal?"

"Local *gal*?" Lee said. This time he sneered outright. "Dude, can I help you with your game here? You sound like my mother. But, yes, she was a local *gal*. You have been gone a long time, haven't you?

"She lives up the hill, as a matter of fact," Lee continued. "A therapist. Actually, she's a terrific lady—sorry, *gal*—if too possessive. In any case, it didn't work out. I wish her well. Life goes on."

He glowered at Sam. "Life just goes on. Right?"

Lee sat back, put his hands behind his head, and, looking straight at Sam, yawned again. "I think you live near her. Adva Sharma? Dr. Adva Sharma?" Lee smiled, but his eyes remained cold and Sam felt violence shimmer off of him.

Sam held on, took a breath, turned his head to the right and nodded at a woman he couldn't even focus on, then returned his attention to Lee. Lee would know if he lied about knowing Adva.

"We met. We're neighbors. Seems nice enough. I don't know much about her. But I'm slightly confused. Isn't she . . . ?"

"A dyke?"

Lee's face darkened and turned down so that his eyes peered up. His mouth had twitched when he'd said, "dyke." It was his turn to recover. He looked Sam in the eyes and shook his head back and forth. Sam held his gaze but forced a look of curiosity.

"Excuse me. A lesbian. Right. Go figure, dude. You never know. Do you?" Lee said. "With these . . . you know."

"With these . . .?"

"Women nowadays. Most of them are psychos. They don't know what they want. But they do know how to get it. They put out and keep their eyes on your wallet." He laughed. "You must have that problem, too, being a writer and all." Laughed again. "What do you write about?"

Sam could barely see straight. Lee's own hatred came out of him like shock waves from an underground explosion. Sophie's face came to the front of his mind. He needed to leave immediately. Instead he said:

"That's . . ."

Sam scoured his mind for the right words. He needed to be American, he needed to be Lee's new friend, and he needed to keep this conversation going. He pulled up some dorm room language from twenty years earlier: "That's . . . fucked up, man. Seriously fucked up. About your wife turning gay."

Lee's face was impossible to read. He pursed his lips a little and tilted his head a fraction of an inch upwards. Sam saw that his neck was well muscled and extremely strong. There was no way Sam could beat him in a one-on-one fight. No matter what, he had to stay calm.

"Right. It wasn't cool," Lee said. "So what do you write about, Sam?"

Taking down Clayborne would take a well-placed bullet, maybe more than one. Sam imagined Lee with bullets in him, still moving, still coming at him. Clayborne, sitting in the red vinyl 1950s retro booth, seemed invincible.

"Wine."

"Wine," Lee repeated. "You write about wine. Interesting. Seems like Paris would be the perfect place to do that. What brought you here?"

The beer, which he'd finished quickly, had gone to Sam's

head. What was Clayborne thinking? He needed to change the subject. If there was ever a time for Sam to lose his decades-long acquired reticence, it was now.

"I think I saw her with her girlfriend," Sam said.

"Who?" Lee asked.

"Your ex. She's with the sculptor, right?" Sam said, his alien voice back. "Older woman? I've seen them around. Strange that your ex threw you over for her. Like you said, women these days."

Lee put both his hands on the back of his side of the booth, then behind his head again, out of sight, nonthreatening.

"You're right about that, my friend," Lee said. "I was tricked. The sexy shrink got me. Then she took my money. Go figure. I'm not the first. I won't be the last."

"She knew you were a catch," Sam said.

Lee laughed loudly. "Let's just say I'll be more careful next time."

A councilwoman colleague of Lee's came in with a date. She introduced him, a lawyer from Shaker Heights. Lee, in turn, introduced them both to Sam. They talked for ten minutes about the presidential primary campaign. The woman was for John McCain, her lawyer friend was for Hillary Clinton. Lee remained neutral; he complimented both candidates, as well as Barack Obama and Mike Huckabee.

"They all have something to offer us," Lee said. "Why do we have to pick a party? May the best man—or woman—win."

After they left, he said, "Idiots. Look, dude, I vote with my wallet. Just point me in the direction of the guy who'll get rid of the estate tax and I'll punch the card. But let's not talk politics. I could care less."

He took a sip of his second martini.

"What about you, Sammy? Married, divorced? What's your deal?"

Sam had prepared for this. Knowing that Lee might have heard gossip or somehow learned something of Sophie in the years since the rape, Sam twisted all aspects of the truth.

He'd renamed Sophie "Kathy," after his childhood next-door neighbor. He'd practiced her name for days. He changed her college to Northwestern, which wasn't too far from where he'd grown up, and a campus he could reference easily, if pressed and anxious. He changed the color of her hair to brown, but if he said blond by mistake, he'd say she'd once colored it. He changed her interests from tennis and piano to cooking. He changed her occupation to food and wine consultant for Air France. If Lee left no stone unturned, Sam wanted to make sure nothing crawled out.

The only thing he kept the same was how much he'd loved her and how she'd died. He described her death from the brain tumor in detail. He left out his belief about the connection between the beating and her tumor.

Sam told him details. He wanted him to know, to have Sophie's painful death in Clayborne's brain, whether it registered tonight or not. Someday it would register, and when it did, Sam wanted to see it happen.

Lee acted genuinely moved when Sam finished his story about Sophie.

"Wow, man," Lee said. "Brutal stuff. You have my sympathy. I'm really sorry."

The two men sat in silence for a while.

"You and your wife lived in Paris?"

Sam's gut tightened into an excruciating knot.

"Yes. Paris. Why?"

"Huh. I think I knew a girl who might have lived in Paris. What was your wife's name, Sam?"

Sam's mind was spinning, his heart hammering. "Kathy. Her name was Kathy."

"Kathy," Lee said. "Funny you never mentioned her name before. Kathy? Kathy Koppang, huh?"

"Right," Sam said. "I called her Kathy. A lot of people called her Katherine, her given name. Katherine was more of a French name, so the French called her that. I called her Kathy. But you know what, Lee? It's hard for me to hear her name, much less say it. Okay? You can understand that, right? I really don't want to go there tonight."

"I won't say her name again. I can understand that. I've had my own heartbreak. Like I said, I'm really sorry, man."

"You mean with your ex-wife?" Sam said. "With Adva?"

"Fuck, no, bro. This was someone I didn't know very well, but there was potential. This was in college. She disappeared."

"What do you mean, she disappeared?"

"She quit school in the middle of the year and split." Lee paused. "Buddy of mine told he saw her in Paris, of all places. Strange, huh? All these people moving to France? Her name was Sophie."

Sam visualized his father. He channeled his calm, Midwestern strength. If he had ever needed that simple power, it was now.

"There were a lot of Sophies in France, Lee. I probably met a few of them. But I don't remember another expat." He stared at Lee, held his gaze. "Maybe Kathy knew her. But I didn't know any Sophies."

"Beautiful girl. You'd remember her. She was hot."

Sam's heart again pounded so hard he could hardly hear his own words.

"I said . . . I may have met some women named Sophie, but I didn't know anyone by that name." Sam's voice rose and his speech grew more rapid. "Kathy may have, like I said. But Kathy spoke good French, and I don't. So no. I don't know, and I didn't know anyone named Sophie."

"Huh," Lee said again. "Still. Weird coincidence, don't you think?"

Sam's rage held him together. He'd come too far to lose it now. He slammed half a beer and his voice grew stronger. "You know what? Enough about sad things. Let's talk about you, Lee. How's business?"

"All right. I do my thing. I'm good at what I do—building houses. But I'm no angel. I'm a normal guy; I make mistakes when I get too passionate about something. Because of that passion, I had a little trouble a while back."

He took a sip of his martini and said, "You seem like the kind who keeps his own counsel, Sam. I want you to keep mine. Can I count on that?"

"Who would I talk to?" Sam said.

"There is a woman in town I care about. I'm crazy about her, to tell you the truth. I'm no professional writer, like you. I'm not a slick guy with words. You are—I mean, you're a writer."

"Okay," Sam said, his rage returning, giving him strength.

"I wonder if you could put in a good word for me."

Sam drank the last of his beer. "Me? How?"

"She works at Whirly's. The owner has had it in for me for years, and he banned me from entering the bar. He can't legally, but I'm not about to take him to court and let him countersue. So I stay away."

"Why don't you call her? Go see her at home?"

"Johnny Kenston—the owner—poisoned her mind about me, told her lots of lies. She's young and impressionable."

Sam responded instantly, buoyantly, if a little too quickly. He remembered a phrase from college.

"You want me to be your wingman. You got it. I expect the same from you, though. I might need some navigational assistance in the woman arena," Sam said. "I'd like to meet someone, too," he lied. He grabbed the check.

"No, no, you don't," Lee said, trying to take the check away from Sam. "My treat. My town. Your euro's no good here, Pierre."

Sam threw a few twenties on the table and stood up. He imagined pointing a gun at Lee's head and pulling the trigger.

"Done," Sam said. "Next one's yours. Make me earn it. I'll even go see this young lady for you. What's her name?"

"Rachel," Lee said. "You can't miss her. Nice curves, black hair. She's there Thursday through Saturday."

Sam wanted to know more about Lee before it was over. Was he abusing this woman, too?

"I'll talk to her. Maybe we can all get together. But I'll need a date. I can't be alone forever, you know what I mean? I'll have to widen my search. I haven't tried the bars around the corner. Which one do you recommend?"

"Try Tommy's Bistro. Some major talent there on the right nights. Monday is Ladies' Night. Go then."

Now it was Sam's turn to laugh a little too loud. "You got it."

Lee was laughing now, too. Lee and Sam walked to the door. The night air had cooled and they stood outside.

"Feels good," Lee said. "It got hot in there."

"Hang tight. I'll talk to this Rachel friend of yours," Sam said. "I need your number. I didn't record it when you called."

"Let's exchange," Lee said. He took out his BlackBerry to punch in Sam's number. He waited. Sam, for the first time all night, was completely lost. He hadn't prepared for this, so defaulted to honesty.

"No phone." He shrugged.

"Where'd you call me from?"

"That phone booth outside the bookstore. In the Village Triangle."

Lee looked at him, cocked his head.

"That thing works? Is this 1958?" His laughter ended in a sneer. "Is my village paying to keep up that piece of shit? I'll have to check on that."

"No, it actually works. I haven't gotten around to getting a new phone yet. Monday I'm going to Solon to buy a cell phone I can use in the States."

"You need a lift?"

"I'm good. I bought a used pickup truck."

"Never ceases to amaze. A Frenchman with no cell phone who drives a pickup truck. I'm guessing you write on an old desktop PC from the nineties. Am I right?"

Sam smiled. "Manual typewriter."

Lee burst out laughing. "No way, dude. This is too good. We should make you the village mascot. 'The Luddite writer.' See you around. Next one's on me."

Lee was impressed. Sam was sophisticated, if not a genuine eccentric artist. There had to be hundreds of wannabe writers in Paris, and more than a few who wrote about wine. He'd been pretty convincing about dead Kathy, whoever the hell she was. More important, he was cooler than Lee's local friends, the sycophants and spoiled rich kids. The Euro expat writer might be a good wingman. Lee could use a sophisticated friend, one with some mileage. It sounded like this guy had been through hell and out the other side. Maybe not caring about a phone or computer was some writer thing. In any case, it didn't matter.

He now had an in with Rachel—a trustworthy person to vouch for him. The new guy in town could be of some use, after all.

He got in his car, turned it on, and stared straight ahead. He looked out of the left side of the car and saw Sam walking up Grove Hill, past Cottage Street, where Adva and Ellen lived, toward his house. He watched Sam disappear after he turned right on Summit Street.

Lee felt the martinis wearing off quickly. Something felt wrong. He didn't like that Sam had paid for the drinks, but that wasn't it. Sam had arrived in town before Christmas. Three and a half months was too long for anyone to go without a phone in 2008. Yet that wasn't it, either.

Then Lee felt as if a knife blade had suddenly been held at his throat. If Sam's dead wife Kathy had known Sophie, then Kathy might have heard about the night in college when Lee had roughed up Sophie. Kathy could have told Sam about it before she died.

But so what if she did? Why would a wine writer leave France and come to Chestnut Falls because of something that happened to a friend of his wife's? That didn't make sense. The only thing that made sense to Lee was if Sam's wife's name hadn't been Kathy. That's when he remembered Sam's face when Lee had said the name "Sophie."

Chapter Thirty-Nine

ADVA AND LEE HAD not spoken since their divorce. With assets divided, the birdcage in Lee's car, and no children to dispute, the moment they walked out of the courtroom they had an unspoken understanding to remain unspeaking.

They rarely saw each other, despite living in a village of barely four thousand people. He crushed his thoughts of her into a black hole of silent hatred and focused on what mattered: Clayborne Homes and the money it would bring him, making him eventually free and clear of his father; sculpting his body in his home gym; and now, Rachel Rosen, his redemption.

Two weeks had passed since he had had drinks with Sam. Lee Clayborne entered his home gym and smelled the organic citrus cleaner used by his Amish cleaning woman. Everything was spotless, including the hi-def TVs in the upper corners of two sides of the rooms. He breathed in the citrus and sat down on a bench of his Hoist machines. He looked at the universal remote control and left it alone and the screens stayed blank. He placed his gloved hands on the bar of the triceps machine and pulled down fifteen times, in the first of three reps.

That Sam Koppang knew Adva hadn't seemed important to Lee when he and Sam had talked over drinks. But in the two weeks since, it had begun to bother him.

He hadn't heard from Koppang since that night. The writer

had promised him—*he had shaken his hand on it*—that he would talk to Rachel on Lee's behalf. That he would make it right.

Since then, not a word.

What if Koppang *had* been married to Sophie? What if he were friends with Adva and not just acquaintances? Maybe they were all laughing at Lee right now. He imagined them sitting in her run-down dump on Cottage Street. The dyke would be there, sharing the joke—laughing at Lee's desire to be with a woman he could really love and who could love him for who he was. Laughing at how easily Lee had trusted Sam.

Lee now believed this: Sam had come to ruin him. To take things from him. Now that he knew his weak spot he'd try to take Rachel. Maybe try to damage his business.

He would deal with the French con artist when the time was right.

As the sweat poured off of him and he watched his muscles strain in the mirror, Lee needed to know about Sam's relationship with Adva. But in a town this small, you didn't go around asking questions. You had to figure it out other ways.

He worked the quad machine. He adjusted the weight and made it heavier.

If Koppang was friends with Adva, then he'd heard the lies about him that Adva would tell. If he combined those with what Sophie might have told him . . .

"This is a cluster-fuck," Lee said out loud. He continued working out.

Would Adva tell Sam sob stories? Would she lie about him and say that she'd been abused physically, sexually, financially, and emotionally? That's what she'd said in a heated argument before the divorce. Adva, with her psychobabble and therapist's double-talk. Lee couldn't stand it.

"Just be a *wife*. Is that so hard?" he'd said to her again and again. If he'd raised his voice, it was because she'd refused to listen.

But, no. She failed him.

Adva would conveniently forget to mention to Sam that it was she who had really been the abuser—by withholding affection, by always asking where he was going, what he was doing, and ultimately taking a woman as a lover. She'd had the nerve to threaten to expose him in court documents if he didn't settle on the usual fifty-fifty split. Lee eventually grew sick of lawyers' fees and told his high-priced, downtown Cleveland dago hotshot to just make it go away.

Lee got off the weight machine. He needed to calm down. Maybe Adva wouldn't complain to Sam. Lee knew Adva too well. She was a coward; she'd wanted their marriage over and had refused to work on keeping them together.

That left only one explanation for Sam's silence, and it was one that sent Lee Clayborne into a dark place he'd only been a few times in his life. This time, he felt himself going farther into it than ever before.

It's not just about a dead wife. It's not about Adva. He's fucking Rachel.

Rachel, impressionable girl that she was, must have bought Sam's lonely widower routine.

Lee needed to remain cool. Tonight he had a council meeting. Afterward he'd walk by Whirly's on his way to J's with his colleagues.

If he didn't see Koppang sniffing around, he'd send in Jeffrey, his toady on council. He'd tell Jeffrey that Koppang was a troublemaker, maybe dangerous, and that Lee needed to know if he was bothering the girl behind the bar. That's all. He just needed confirmation. It was Thursday night—traditional singles' night in The Bubble—and the bar would be crowded. Rachel would be there.

Lee finished his bench presses on the free weights. He got on the treadmill. He tore off his T-shirt. He looked in the mirror. His body astonished even him. Under the recessed lighting, his muscles were beautiful this afternoon. He watched them move up and down, as if they were a fluid work of art. He began to laugh, a chuckle at first, then harder, full throated.

"Yes!" he shouted. He pumped his fist into the air. "Yes, yes, yes, yes!"

He had figured it out. He wasn't going to be a victim again. He would destroy anyone who got between him and his new woman.

Chapter Forty

ADVA AND SAM SAT in the Popcorn Shop. Early May in North-eastern Ohio could mean rain or even sleet. Today it meant balmy breezes and filtered sunlight through wispy cirrus clouds.

"This smells nice. Maybe Ellen would like this coffee," Adva said, stirring in the milk. She looked out the window. "You're right. It's a lovely view. This is a town landmark and I've never been here. I thought it was a tourist spot."

"It's a nice place to write sometimes," Sam said.

The view from the high round table overlooked the natural falls on the west side of the river, just south of the Town Hall.

"Adva."

"Yes, Sam." She smiled. She looked relaxed, if a little tired.

"You know I'm pretty solitary."

"No kidding." She smiled.

"But I'm human."

"This is quite a day for revelations."

When Sam didn't smile, she asked, "What's going on?"

"I need to tell you something. I care about you, and there's something that you need to know. Something I did. I don't want you to find out from someone else."

"Okay." She put her coffee down.

"I had drinks with him, Adva."

Her eyes widened but she said nothing.

Over the entrance, a bell rang as a young family entered.

The father pushed open the heavy old wooden door. A mother and three small children came inside. The family of five all had various shades of blond hair and they jostled their way into the shop. The children chattered and gestured at the displays. They touched the candies, the popcorn tins, the hats and T-shirts with the store's logo as Sam and Adva watched.

"I wonder sometimes about having children. Ellen doesn't want any. Why would she?" Adva said. She gave a weak smile. "I mean, really, Sam. Why? She has a nice life. She's been through a lot. She doesn't want a child, and doesn't care what anyone thinks."

"What about you?" Sam said, relieved Adva was reacting so calmly.

Adva sat up straighter; Sam started: of course he'd been wrong. She wasn't calm, but had just been in momentary shock.

"Why would you *meet* with *him*? I cannot, for the life of me, begin to think of any reason. You know what he did to me."

She looked at the falls. The young family chose their ice-cream cones and popcorn, drinks and souvenirs. Sam heard the mother talking to the manager of the shop. They were from Rocky River, across Cuyahoga County, to the west. In Chestnut Falls for a family reunion, they were getting an early start on the weekend, staying with her husband's mother in town.

"I know what he did to you."

Adva's eyes burrowed into Sam's. "Then why?"

"He thinks we're friends. At least he did two weeks ago. I haven't followed up since then."

"You haven't . . ." Adva shut her eyes. Sam felt a wave of affection for her, different from what he felt for Ellen. Ellen had comforted him. He wanted to comfort Adva. Despite her profession, she was more vulnerable than Ellen, he thought.

"I need to tell you something else, Adva."

The Popcorn Shop played Tin Pan Alley music from a local old-timers' radio station. Sinatra sang "Just the Way You Look Tonight."

"Give me a minute," she said. "I like this song. I want to listen to it before you upset me even more."

"Why I came to town . . ."

"Please, Sam. I really mean it. I want to listen to this song. Get a refill. Please."

Sam got up and put a dollar down for the refill and the manager filled it up. He walked back to the table overlooking the falls. The song finally finished and another started; Count Basie played "April in Paris."

In the moments of the first sixteen bars, they looked at each other and felt Sam's loss. Sam knew, and Alva imagined, what this song had meant to him years before. He and Sophie had had too few Aprils in Paris. Now he sat here, so far from Paris, so very far from Sophie.

"I don't think I'm prepared to deal with what you're going to tell me."

"It's him, Adva."

"Lee Clayborne."

"Yes."

"What about him?"

Sam's throat constricted. He wanted to run out of the door and leave behind the tinkling bell over the Popcorn Shop door, and the flowers that were beginning to bloom all over town, and the easy sunshine outside, and his brick-and-beam office over the hardware store. He wanted to drive his truck to the airport and leave it there. He wanted to leave this place forever, fly back to Paris and forget everything. The air in The Bubble was getting rancid, but it was he who contributed most, with the fetid hatred Erasmo had warned him about.

"*What about Lee?*"

"Sophie."

Adva sat silent and motionless. She looked at Sam and then at her coffee, and then at the falls, then back at Sam.

"I need to ask you something very serious, Sam. You can't screw with me here. Okay?"

"Of course."

"I like you very much. So does Ellen. You're important to us. I don't let people into my personal life lightly. Do you follow me so far?"

"Yes."

"I need to ask you . . . I need to ask you if you are, in any way . . . not healthy. If you are being treated, or were treated, for depression. For bipolar disorder. For anything. Sam: I need to ask if you are delusional. Because this is alarming. I'm scared, you're scaring me, and if you have a problem, I can help you find help."

"Wait. Adva."

"I'm listening. But first you answer."

"No. None of those things. I'm a mess, but not those things. That I know of, anyway."

She looked at him for a long time.

"Should I believe you? My ex and your late wife?"

"They knew each other in college. They were together then."

"He knew her in Paris, too?"

"No."

"Then what are you saying? Are you saying he just knew her? If he just knew her . . . What are you implying?"

"That he hurt her."

"What in the world are you talking about?" Adva's voice was rising.

"He raped her. He beat her for a long time. He beat her head against a floor, a wall . . ."

Sam looked down, then out the window at the falls. Finally he looked at Adva, who had not taken her wide eyes off of his face.

"This is a mistake. I shouldn't have asked you to come here. I should have left well enough alone. Let's leave," Sam said.

"Oh, no. You're going to tell me why you came here." She put her hand on his arm and squeezed. "Please don't get up."

Sam sighed. His stomach began to unwind a little. He felt his life unwinding. He looked at the falls, at the river. It was moving deep and fast over the falls today. He could hear it. The river rushed to the larger Cuyahoga and through that river to Lake Erie and eventually to the Atlantic Ocean. Back home. Away from here. This wasn't home. Home was with Sophie.

"I came to this town because I needed to see his face."

"Sam, I'm horrified to tell you I don't doubt this. Are you saying you think his actions caused her tumor?"

"Yes."

"And you believe that."

"I know it. I'm certain. So was she; so was our doctor. So are a lot of doctors. How can a person's head be smashed over and over like that without serious damage? He did it to her, Adva. I'm sure of it. He killed her, slowly."

For more than an hour, Sam told Adva more details—of Sophie's and his meeting and love affair, their marriage, of their times at Café Virgile, of the big tree at le parc Monceau under which they'd married.

He told her of Sophie's illness, how quickly the tumor took

her. How the old French doctor said her tumor was from a previous trauma, and how Sophie instinctively knew it was true and then he did, too.

Sam told Adva how, at the end, Sophie told him she had to forgive someone, and that Sam thought it was him she had to forgive, for he had withheld love from her at the beginning. "No," Sophie had said, and managed to laugh. "It isn't you, Sam. I've never had to forgive you. It's someone else. It's someone who hurt me."

He described how Sophie had told him more about Lee, and how she needed to forgive him before she died. How she had made Sam promise to find happiness. He did not tell Adva that when he'd promised Sophie in his moment of sorrow, she had already died.

The sun was setting. Sam realized that the Village Council meeting would start in forty-five minutes.

Adva had remained quiet until he finished.

"Now listen to me," she said. "I'm going to tell you about him, and I'm going to make it easy to hear."

She paused, looked at the falls, then at Sam.

"They—men like him—they work on your weakness. If you're insecure, they build you up. They hook you in and then they go after you. The one thing they cannot abide, Sam, is rejection. I've no doubt—none—that somehow she rejected him. So he beat and raped her. That's who and what he is. You could get a PhD, but that's all you really need to know. I've been dealing with this a long time. I expect I always will. These people—and they are almost always men, Sam—they can be very dangerous. Sam, what have you gotten yourself into?"

Adva stopped talking and glanced out of the window. She looked again into Sam's eyes.

"But I've moved on. So I'm going to ask you again: *What are you doing here?*"

Sam stared at his coffee, which was empty. He looked around at nothing.

"Are you here for revenge?"

"Adva."

"Because if you are here for revenge, of some kind, in some way, this will not end well, Sam. It would be the worst thing you could possibly do. And Sam, you . . . you're not cut out for it. He is . . . how can I say this . . . he will always be a step ahead of you. Revenge is wrong in any event . . . and he would destroy you first."

Adva paused. Sam stayed quiet.

"Does Lee know about you? Why you're here?"

"No, of course not."

"You're sure of this, Sam?"

"I think I'm sure. How could he know?"

"Sam, where have you been for the past fifteen years? There's the Internet. Was there a death notice in *Le Monde*? Anything that he could look up? Something he could have found, something that ties you to Sophie?"

"I suppose so. I don't remember, Adva. He said he had a friend who met Sophie in Paris."

"Oh my God, Sam. Were you with her then?"

"Yes, but I told him it wasn't me. I told him I was married to a woman named Katherine."

"Oh my God. Listen to me, Sam. Lee is clever, Sam. He's not afraid of anything. I never once saw him anxious or worried. He is calculating and cool in that way, Sam. Much cooler than you."

She looked at her watch.

"Oh, Sam. This is a disaster. But I have to go, and so I need you to . . . I want you to stay here, to not go back to the hot little village in the south of France and be a hermit again."

"Sometimes it's cool. Cold even." Sam finally smiled but it quickly faded.

"Dammit, Sam! You know what I mean. You'll die there. If you are to stay here, you must heal from this. And you must do as I have done, and Sophie did. You must forgive. And stay away from Lee. He's older now, with more to lose. He won't come after you unless you do something to him. Stay away, please." She paused. "I have to go. I have nothing more to say about this."

Sam stood up. Adva, clearly drained, stood up too.

"Thank you," he said.

They hugged.

"We share a great sorrow now, Sam," Adva said, softening.

Sam looked at Adva. Her ink-black hair was down around her shoulders. She looked more Indian to him than she ever had, with her long, straight nose, her arching eyebrows, her wide mouth.

How could Clayborne have done those things to her? To Sophie? He thought of Rachel. Was she next?

They left the Popcorn Shop.

"Walk me home, okay?"

"I'm going to do some writing at my office. It helps me calm down." He paused and said, "Do you want to come up to my office?"

Both of them, at the same moment, from sorrow or helplessness or attraction, from a cocktail of emotions, felt a rush through their groins, a flood of pheromones, a quickening of hearts, a mild sickness in their stomachs from the inevitability, from what was about to happen.

Neither spoke as they crossed the street. Sam felt dizzy. Adva did not think, would not think.

Sam used his key to open the rickety door next to the hardware store. They walked up the stairs, saying nothing; Sam opened the door to his office and turned to the left, to the outer office that had an old leather sofa in it. Standing face to face, they looked into one another's eyes without smiling.

Sam and Adva kissed softly, then harder. He touched her shoulders, back, ran his fingers across the top of her ass. She stroked his neck, then suddenly grabbed for his penis. He instantly knew he had been wrong—he hadn't lost desire. He stroked her vagina and it was very wet and he was very hard and they were quickly through with foreplay. She glanced at the old, dusty sofa and whispered, "Floor" and he was inside her as they hit the floor. They rocked side to side on the ancient wood. She climbed on him and came. She bent her head and licked his neck and lips and they flipped over and no longer cared about the hard floor. They kissed hard and then he came inside of her. He rolled off of Adva and they lay on the floor for a long time until their sweat dried. Adva got dressed, went into the bathroom, and washed her face and hands and tried to fix her hair. She walked to Sam, who was standing naked, and they kissed for a long time without saying a word.

Adva left Sam's office. They did not say good-bye. She walked down the stairs, turned right out of the door onto Main Street, and walked home, where Ellen waited for her.

Chapter Forty-One

SAM DRESSED AND SAT for a while on the sofa and thought about Adva and how he still wanted her. Guilt and desire and fatigue washed through him and there was no getting around it. He walked to his desk, where a bottle of a 2005 red Tuscan he was supposed to write about sat. As Sam poured, its Sangiovese nose reached him. He tasted and typed his notes: *black cherry, chocolate, long finish, balanced.*

He abandoned the writing. He could no longer think of words for wine. He opened the blinds just enough to have a view, and turned the slats slightly up so no one could see in from below.

Across the street from Sam's window, Lee Clayborne parallel parked his car in front of the Town Hall. Sam watched from his office window as Lee talked on his cell phone and laughed. Every now and then he threw his head back in delight at whatever was being said to him, or whatever he was saying.

Sam held the sides of his typewriter. Lee got out of his car and walked to the bottom of the red brick building's worn stone stairs, where three of his colleagues had gathered. He moved one step above them, turned, and began talking.

Sam had a clear view. For a moment he regretted not learning to shoot with Ellen. Then again, whom was he kidding? Did he expect to shoot Clayborne with a handgun from a second-floor window across the street, about seventy-five feet away? He'd never shot at anything, much less aimed or even held a pistol. Wasn't hating him enough? He had to let it go. He could not let it go.

He watched Lee smiling, laughing, maybe joking around, or listening to his colleagues' stories of their personal lives, or their concerns about the village's business. Lee focused his eyes intently on each of them. It seemed to Sam they all liked Lee. Could this really be the same man who did those things to Sophie and Adva?

Lee put his hand on a male colleague's shoulder and entered the Town Hall through one of the high, thick wooden nineteenth-century doors. Lee seemed desperate for attention.

I'll give him the attention he deserves, Sam thought.

Sam's eyes moved upward to the old weather vane on the Town Hall's spire.

Everything is connected in this town, Sam thought. *It's more than a bubble; it's its own world, one I don't belong in.*

Yet this mostly kind and generous town, had somehow nurtured and harbored Lee Clayborne.

Sam's eyesight fell from the spire to the door of the Town Hall as it opened. There, in uniform, was Sergeant Michael Shield. He stood midway down the steps, where Clayborne had been minutes before.

The sergeant in police blues but wearing no hat, ran his hand across his crew cut. Looking around, Shield pulled a cigar from his breast pocket. He took out a lighter and lit it. He drew in the smoke and let it out in a smoke ring. From behind the blinds Sam felt the warmth of friendship. How betrayed Mike would feel when Sam did what he wanted to do.

Sam recalled what Shield told him over dinner last Christmas—that he had the job of turning on and off the recorder for the Council's proceedings, a job he loathed, but part of his deal with the chief. He was there every month. Maybe the chief knew that the former big-city cop wasn't just good for the village, but the village and its business was good for him too.

Sam squinted and moved his face closer to the window. It was unmistakable. Even at a Village Council meeting, Sergeant Michael Shield carried his gun.

Sam knew what he had to do—kill Clayborne when he came out of the next meeting. Now he had three things to deal with. He had to get his own gun. He had to avoid shooting Michael Shield at all costs. And he didn't want his friend to have to shoot him.

Chapter Forty-Two

Michael shield stood across the street from the hardware store and Sam's office.

"Evening, Mike," Sam called across the street. "Working overtime?"

Sam turned back around and locked the old door to the narrow stairway up to his office.

"Hello, pal," Shield shouted back. "The usual—the last-Thursday-of-the-month gig. The singles set and the politicians. Looking for the same thing, if you catch my drift." He gave an exaggerated wink and smiled.

Sam smiled and jaywalked across Main Street. He calculated how long the meeting would last, how long Clayborne would remain inside, presiding over Council.

"Have a smoke?" Shield asked Sam. "I have another one." He tapped his breast pocket, and without waiting for an answer, he, took out a second cigar and began to unwrap it.

"Can't, Mike," Sam said. His mind went blank so he said the first thing that came to it. "I'm meeting Adva and Ellen at Whirly's," he said.

He hated lying to Shield, but he couldn't use the excuse of going home. The sergeant knew his home was barren and would question why he'd go back there on a beautiful night.

Shield took a long puff and blew it out away from Sam, then

put the partially unwrapped cigar back in his pocket. "Another time, then."

Shield seemed relaxed, happy even. "I don't want to keep you. But do you have a couple of minutes?"

"How long is . . . ? Is that your political meeting in there? The one you have to—"

"Do nothing at?" Shield said. "Yeah. But nights like this aren't so bad. You feel spring coming?"

"The light is lovely," Sam said. "Springtime, yes."

He had to engage. He couldn't just walk away from his friend.

Shield blew out cigar smoke. His friend's life, Sam sensed, was a peaceful one. He was working in a safe little town. His wife was waiting at home. Mike and Margie just wanted to live out their lives peacefully, to be in love, to have a few friends, to stay near the village in body and mind.

"It seems like a long time since you and I met. That night before Christmas; up the hill?" Shield said.

"A lot's happened."

Why did Sam say that? It had slipped out. He tried to think of a joke to make about it: *Obviously, I'm kidding*, he'd need to somehow say.

"Really? Anything I should know about?" Shield said, and smiled. "A woman, perhaps? Are those ladies you're meeting matchmakers? I'd guess they run with a pretty sophisticated crowd. Can I guess? An arty type? Maybe a lady writer?"

Sam looked at the retired detective's craggy, hopeful face and lied again.

"Something like that, Mike."

"Thought so," Shield said, and nodded.

"Someday I'd like what you and Margie have."

He thought: *I had what you and Margie have. I had it and someone took it from me. He's in the building behind you.*

Shield glanced back at the closed white doors of the red brick town hall. What if the meeting ended early?

Sam couldn't take a chance. Before Shield could turn back around Sam began walking north, toward Whirly's, but looking backwards.

"Michael, I'm late. Can't keep the ladies waiting. Stop in and join us?"

He took that chance that his friend would say no, that Shield would want to get home to Margie right after he locked up the Town Hall. If not, he'd figure something out—say he got the date wrong. Shield would believe him, a writer with no date book, no watch, no cell phone.

"I'd like that."

Sam began to panic; he had so little stomach for deceit—a decade with Sophie had nearly dissolved his ability to lie. The sooner he got this all over with, the better.

"I'll take a rain check, though," Shield said. "But how about next week, okay? Bring your new lady friend."

Sam, now fifty feet away, halfway to Whirly's, turned and called out, "We'll do that, Mike."

"Congratulations, by the way," Shield said.

"On what?" Sam said.

"On moving on a little. On trying. I know it's not easy."

The door to the Town Hall swung open. Shield, distracted now by the group of politicians coming out of the hall, walked inside.

Passing him, bumping him on the shoulder lightly, accidentally it seemed, was a man whom Sergeant Michael Shield despised.

He knew the man had harassed his daughter Amanda's best friend, Rachel, but could do nothing unless Rachel filed a complaint, which she was afraid to do. He knew Lee had abused Adva Sharma, Ellen's partner, whom he knew only as a gentle soul, a good person, a respected psychologist. She'd never called the cops on him, but Shield knew what a bum Clayborne had been to her. He knew Lee Clayborne, like a lot of bad guys, was good at keeping his misdeeds hushed up.

Shield wanted to grab Clayborne by the collar and throw him down the worn stone stairway. He wanted to put him on the sidewalk and do what he had done a few times in New York, as a last resort, when the law wouldn't work and he couldn't stand by. He wanted to shove him down and kick him in the ribs, then stand him up and break his nose. Shove him down again, and when he begged Shield to stop, kick him in his groin. As Clayborne lay gasping for breath, Shield would give him a variation on the few off-duty verbal lessons he'd given to men who hurt women: *If I hear one more thing about you bothering that woman, you'll wish you were never born. Next time I won't be so nice.*

It wasn't original, but it had been effective back in the day, or so Michael Shield liked to tell himself. The problem now was that he was too old. And they weren't in the City, they were in The Bubble. So instead he said: "Excuse me, Mr. Clayborne."

Chapter Forty-Three

DURING THE NEXT TWO weeks, Sam took his walks. He drove to Pennsylvania, to Chet's store, and talked football, baseball, a little hockey, and always wine. He wrote two wine reviews. He chatted with Jimmy Schultz. He went over to Mike Shield's house and had a few beers and watched the Indians play the Yankees on TV. Sam told Mike about his youthful passion for the Chicago White Sox, how he'd taken his pop to a Mets game. When he told Mike about how Pop said he liked the Mets because they were underdogs, Shield didn't laugh.

"Not a Mets fan myself," Mike replied. Sam didn't mention it again. *Merde, these Yankee fans*, Sam thought and smiled to himself. *They never change.*

His smile faded and his blood went cold: *Double life*. That's what he led. Somehow, maybe Mike would understand the other life he was leading, that of a stalker, a killer; but of course he couldn't tell him. He needed to find a way to keep Mike out of whatever he was going to do, however he was going to do it.

Ellen and Adva left for ten days to visit friends in Madison, Wisconsin, then hang out for a few days in Chicago. They'd left a lighthearted note for Sam, with the keys to their house and instructions on feeding and watering Ringo. He'd come to like the big dog, and the dog liked him.

One afternoon, toward mid-May, walking to the post office from his office to mail his review to his editor in New York, Sam saw Lee Clayborne sitting in his SUV at a traffic light.

"I owe you a call," Sam shouted to him. "Can we get together?"

Lee Clayborne stared at Sam, his face blank but for a slight narrowing of his eyes, and said nothing. When the light turned green, he drove on.

Sam had taken the chance that Clayborne would not come for him—that he hadn't connected him with Sophie. The look on Clayborne's face shook that belief. He'd finally seen the face that Sophie and Adva had seen: the face of a man who no longer cared to impress. He saw the face of a dangerous man who wanted very badly to hurt him.

The day before Adva and Ellen were to return from Chicago, after walking and feeding Ringo, Sam let himself into Adva's studio. He'd seen the gun case when she'd given him the tour of their home. He had the key to it on the key chain they'd given him. He tried the smallest key, and it worked. He opened the case and looked at Ellen's .22 rifle. He touched it. It belonged to Ellen. It was her connection to her father, to one of the only things in her youth that had empowered her. He took his hand away from the gun.

Sam locked the case back up, left the studio, took the keys off his key chain, and put them in an empty flowerpot by the back door, on the deck. He walked up the hill, went inside his house, grabbed the keys to his truck, and left through the front door.

Chapter Forty-Four

On the drive to Pennsylvania Sam didn't want to think about Lee Clayborne. His face had looked utterly different to Sam. Lee knew something . . . but what? A little, a lot, everything? To get Lee's face out of his mind, he recalled details from his days with Sophie, just as he had done under the ceiling fan as it turned like constellations in Ville de Rachat, lost in his mist of wine and grief. There he could leave the grief behind for a few hours and enjoy moments of tenderness from their time together. Today, driving, letting his mind wander, he could smell her, feel his fingertips on her skin, imagine her voice. Through the light rain of late May, Sam drove and remembered. Three times he smiled. Once he laughed.

Sam pulled into the gravel parking lot of the store where he usually bought his cigarettes or coffee or juice for the ride back. It had stopped raining. In the mountains the clouds hung low and dark gray.

So much gray, yet different from Paris gray. Sam recalled an essay by Saul Bellow, who wrote of "Baudelaire's Parisian sky weighing the city down like a heavy pot lid." Sam came to agree with Bellow, who said that he was "such a sucker for its tones of gray." Yet Sam had come to see the colors in the gray, the oranges and golds and pinks and greens and purples. Had Bellow, too, come to see warmth in a color that was cold?

Were the colors really there, or did I see them because of Sophie?

After Sophie died, Sam had seen only gray, flat and impenetrable gray. When Paris became unbearably gray, he left for Ville de Rachat, where there were colors that penetrated his eyes, if not his heart.

Sam stood under the slate gray skies in the rainy western Pennsylvania mountains and felt only the rain.

He went inside the store. Sam was relieved to see Chet.

"How you doon', Sam," Chet said. "It's been a little while. Pack of smokes? Carton today? What else you need?" he said, turning toward the cigarette display behind him. "I got some of that Le Coq Rouge you'ns was talking about. Bought a case, took some home to my wife." He laughed his phlegmy smoker's cough. "It got me a good reception."

"No smokes today, Chet. Glad your wife liked it."

"They got to you, too?" Chet said. "You quit? You'ns are killing me. Gonna put me out of business."

He smiled. He wore a Pittsburgh Steelers jersey with the number twelve and "Bradshaw" on the back.

"I remember him," Sam said, nodding at Chet's jersey. "He beat up my Bears pretty bad."

"Well the Bears doan bother me. The Browns—I do love beating up on them Browns. So, Sam. What can I do you for?"

"I need something, Chet. I'm hoping you can help me."

Chet looked at Sam closely. He'd never taken Sam for a druggie. He didn't think he needed to tell him he didn't deal dope.

Sam looked around to make sure no one else was in the store.

"What is it, Sam?" Chet said.

"You know I've been living in Europe, right, Chet?"

"That I do."

"What I didn't tell you . . ." Sam hesitated.

Chet tensed. When he didn't know where a conversation was going, he calculated how fast he could get to the shotgun under the counter. Maybe he'd misread his new friend the wine writer.

"I didn't mention that I had problems with a crazy person in Europe."

"I'm sorry to hear that."

Chet figured two seconds—one to aim, one more to pull the trigger.

"And that crazy person may have followed me here. Actually, to Ohio."

Chet remained silent but began to relax. Sam sounded tentative and legitimately afraid of something, or someone.

"I need to protect myself."

"I'm not sure I understand you, Sam."

"I need to protect myself, Chet. But I don't want to go through the hassle, the . . ."

Confirmed. He wasn't lying. Chet began to nod his head.

"The bullshit of background checks and the waiting period," Chet said. "Am I right?"

"It's not as if I've done anything wrong. I don't have a record, Chet. I'm a peaceful man. I just need to protect myself."

"We all need that. I own at least a dozen guns. Pretty much everybody around here has more guns than I do."

"So you understand."

"But I'm not a gun dealer. Why you asking me?"

"Okay, of course. I'm sorry, Chet. I just thought . . ."

"I'm not a gun dealer."

"Yes, Chet, I heard you. I understand."

"And you're okay with that? What are you gonna do? You can

go to a pawnshop, you know. There's one down there toward Pittsburgh."

"I'm sure I'll be fine."

Chet stopped moving and put his hands on the counter.

"Somebody's after you, but you're sure you'll be fine. Someone might kill you but you can wait a day to protect yourself. Is that what you're telling me, Sam?"

Sam took a deep breath. "No one can be sure of anything, Chet. But I'm sure as I can be."

There was a long pause.

"I'll just take a cup of coffee," Sam said. "I wonder if we could just forget this. I'm overreacting. My imagination got the better of me on the drive here."

Sam wondered if Chet would report him, if he would call the highway patrol or the local cops. He had to cut his losses as fast as possible. He'd never felt farther away from France—from home.

Chet walked over to the front door. He turned the "Open" sign over. He locked the door and turned back to Sam.

"I'll open it back up. My customers are used to my irregular hours."

Chet remained in front of the counter. He looked at a door with a small sign that said "Employees Only" and nodded at it.

"Back room."

He began walking, Sam following him. Then he stopped and turned around.

"But first look me in the eye."

Sam did.

"Tell me you understand that we never had this conversation. That if anything happens, and you talk about where you got it, I can't guarantee bad things won't happen to you, Sam. I don't mean by the police. There are things out of my control. My suppliers aren't sentimental. But I like you, Sam, and I don't want you to screw yourself up. Okay?"

He breathed out heavily. Sam smelled the cigarettes and beer on his breath.

"I'm giving you a break."

Chet ran his hand across his nearly bald head.

"Maybe I don't know you. You're a guy who's been living in a country I don't like, no offense, who writes about ridiculously expensive wine. I like learning about it, but it's still strange to me, to say the least. The whole goddamn thing. Okay? But I like you."

"This never happened, Chet."

Chet looked around his store. It was all he had. It was his life, the store and his wife. There were still lots of medical bills from when his wife had almost died of breast cancer, five years earlier. He knew Sam's wife had died. That's all he really knew about him; but that was enough to make them brothers.

"Okay," Chet said.

Chet walked to the back room doorway and opened it and motioned Sam inside.

"I hope you brought cash."

The back room was tidy and bright. Shelves were neatly labeled, store supplies were lined and stacked, and there was no clutter. Sam looked for signs of another, more foreboding room, or a safe. There was nothing that he could see.

In the back left corner of the room was a beige metal desk. Where Sam expected to see grime and dust, he saw an unclut-tered surface with a black wire rack for files: "Food Suppliers,"

"Beverage Suppliers," "Receivables," "Bills," "Things to Do." He smelled a pine cleaning solution and saw a spray bottle of cleaner.

"Nice office," he said.

Chet ignored this and sat down at his desk. He reached down and took his key chain off his belt, which was loose around his waist. He fingered through the key chain and found the key he was looking for, then opened the bottom right-hand drawer.

Sam couldn't see what he was looking at, but Chet was studying the contents of the drawer. Finally he reached down and took out an object covered with red cheesecloth.

Sam smelled something unfamiliar.

"Gun oil," Chet said.

He put the heavy cheesecloth on the neat, tan metal desk.

"Now," he said. "I've chosen for you. You obviously don't know what you're doing, so I'm taking the liberty. You cool with that, Sam the Chicago Bears fan?"

"Thank you, Chet," Sam said.

Chet unwrapped the cheesecloth. He picked up a gun and held it flat in his hand.

"Sit there," he said, nodding to the chair on the other side of his desk.

"You've heard of a .38 special?"

Sam didn't respond. "Sam, you've heard of a .38 special, right?"

Sam looked at the gun. It reminded him of toy guns he'd played with as a boy.

"I'm sure I have."

"That's what this is. It's not a snub-nose. It's no Saturday night special, made-in-China piece of shit. It's a real gun, a serious gun, a beautiful gun. This one is probably from the mid-1970s."

Chet pushed the ejector pin and opened the barrel, showed it to Sam, and spun it. Sam saw that the chambers were empty. Chet pointed the gun away from Sam and pulled the trigger. Then he shut the chamber in one quick motion.

"It's empty," he said. "But it holds six bullets . . . if you have to load it. Think 'six-shooter,' like when we was kids. You look nervous, Sam."

"I've just never—"

"You've never been around guns. I never would have guessed." Chet looked at Sam.

"All right. This is a Model 10, Smith & Wesson Police Special. It's a simple, perfect revolver. This isn't a semiautomatic. But it's double action. Watch."

Chet pointed the gun away from Sam again and cocked the trigger.

"If you cock it, it fires faster and more accurately. There's no movement, no jerking."

He pulled the trigger. Chet's hand was rock steady.

"But you can fire away if you need to." Chet fired four times in a row. "And you don't need to cock it. Less accurate but still fast. Do you understand?"

"I always wondered why they did that on TV. The cocking thing. I thought it was for effect," Sam said.

Chet put the gun down.

"This is serious business," he said.

"Of course. I'm sorry."

"Take it," Chet said. "Hold it."

Sam took the gun by the handle. It was wood, the color of brown shoe polish. Its pebbled stock felt solid and natural in his hand. He thought it would be heavier.

"Look at the bottom of the handle."

Sam turned it over. Where once there had been the letter

D followed by six numbers, there was a smooth, shiny metal surface.

"The serial number is ground off," Chet said. "Ground real deep, deep enough so that it's completely gone."

Sam didn't respond.

"This is an untraceable piece."

"I understand," Sam said.

"Now point it over there and fire it."

Sam turned the gun around, held it, and cocked the trigger. He pulled the trigger.

"Now fire it a few times."

Sam pulled the trigger six times.

"Surprisingly easy," Sam said without smiling.

Chet took the gun back and pushed the ejector pin and opened the barrel. "I'm going to show you how to load it. Don't be nervous. We're not going to shoot anything."

He took out one bullet from his desk drawer and, in one quick motion, put it in the chamber and slapped the chamber shut. Sam's hands began to sweat.

"See?" Chet said, looking in Sam's face. "You can do that, right?"

"Yes."

Chet opened the chamber and emptied the round into his hand and put it back in his desk drawer, then shut the chamber.

"You think you can do that?"

"Yes. It looks easy," Sam said.

"Never load this unless you intend to use it."

Chet looked at Sam and remembered that Sam's wife had died, and that Sam was a drinker.

"Give me your word."

"About?"

"Give me your word that you'll never use this on yourself. That you're using it for self-protection."

"You have my word."

Chet wrapped the .38 in the red cheesecloth.

"Price?" Sam said.

"It's five hundred dollars. I'm giving it to you for four. That's no bullshit. I feel worried about you. But that's my lowest offer and it's not negotiable."

Sam took out his wallet and counted out four hundred dollars. His hands were shaking. He looked up and smiled at Chet.

"I'm a little hungry, I guess. Tired and shaky."

"Buy a sandwich for the way home," Chet said. "And coffee. Because Sam: do not, do not, *do not* get pulled over on your way home. Under any circumstances. The cops will take one look at you and they'll know something's wrong and ask too many questions."

"Okay. Thank you."

They both rose. Chet put the .38 in a paper bag and then wrapped the paper bag in a plastic bag. They walked out of the office and Chet put a package of potato chips in the plastic bag, making sure it was sticking out enough to be seen. He put a roast beef sandwich in another plastic bag, along with a napkin. He poured a large coffee and gave it to Sam, who now held two bags and coffee.

"You be careful not to spill it."

"Thank you, Chet. You might have saved my life."

He tried to stick his hand out.

"No problem," Chet said. "We can shake hands next time. You can pay for the food next time, too. You forgetting something?"

"I really appreciate this, and I won't get pulled over."

Chet reached underneath the counter and took out a box of fifty cartridges, .38 Special. He added it to the bag with the gun and the potato chips.

Sam nodded and headed to the door, juggling the bags to open it.

"You have no idea what you're doing, do you, Sam?" Chet shook his head.

Sam tried to figure out what to say. By the time he turned around to reply, Chet had gone back into his office and Sam stared into an empty store.

Chapter Forty-Five

EARLIER IN THE DAY, clouds and rain had moved east past
Chestnut Falls and through neighboring Geauga and Ashtabula
Counties, then on into Pennsylvania. Sam drove west through
and under them.

As he passed the Ohio line on his drive home the skies had
begun to clear. By the time he arrived in the Village of Chestnut
Falls the sky was cloudless, the occluded front had cleared out
and was heading for the East Coast. By tomorrow it would be
raining in New York City, but now there were clear skies from
Chestnut Falls to Wyoming. The forecast for Thursday night
through the weekend was for ideal weather—seventy degrees,
low humidity, no clouds.

Sam turned into his driveway, got out of his truck, and
was enveloped in the softness of the mid-May evening.
Empty-handed, he closed the truck door and walked to the spot
where he'd first met Michael Shield and had seen the Christmas
lights of Chestnut Falls.

Just past the hardware store building and his office, Riverside
Park was again covered in lights. The Jaycees had draped a huge
maple tree, the hardware store building, the Town Hall, and
the Popcorn Shop in miniature white lights for Blossom Time,
the rite-of-spring festival that took place every Memorial Day
weekend, beginning on the Thursday night of the holiday. The

festival's partially built Ferris wheel reflected the harsh yellow glare of larger construction lights.

Sam crossed Main Street and sat against the old stone WPA wall that five months earlier had reminded him of England. He fixed his eyes on the lights, grew drowsy in the warming evening, and dozed off.

Soon a car drove up Grove Hill and the driver honked the horn, waking him from his short sleep. Honking was a custom that had taken hold in the village decades ago, after one too many crashes at the three-way stop at the top of the hill.

Sam stood up and crossed the street. He opened the passenger door of the truck and took out the package containing potato chips and a handgun.

The unlocked front door to his house was already opened by a few inches. He froze, then forced himself to breathe and prepared for his confrontation with Lee Clayborne, who, he was certain, waited in his kitchen.

Sam put the package from Chet's store on the front step. He removed the chip bag quickly, then realized there were no bullets in the gun. He pulled the cheesecloth off the .38, and held the gun by the barrel, to use it as a bludgeoning weapon. He opened the door and took five long steps into the kitchen: No one there.

The house felt empty to Sam. There was no sound but for his own heartbeat in his ears. He had two choices: search every room and closet, or go with his instinct, which told him he was alone in the house.

Confused, he split the difference.

"Hello," he said, as if a killer would answer him. "Hello!"

There was no answer. He sat down at the kitchen table and placed the gun where he could reach it.

In the ambient light of the Blossom Time decorations and
rides that the Jaycees and carnival workers were putting up,
filtered through his south-facing window, Sam saw an envelope
on his table with his name on it.

He put the gun on the table and sat down. He picked up the
envelope. His name was written in a hand that looked familiar
and feminine. Next to the envelope was different handwriting
on the back of a white cash receipt from the hardware store that
looked masculine and unfamiliar.

The back of the receipt read:

Sam—I hope you don't mind that I put this on your table.
When I knocked, the door swung upon. By the way—lock
your door. You're in America now, my friend. —Mike
Shield

Sam put the receipt down and opened up the sealed envelope. It was a card with two cartoon bears hugging, one light
brown and one pink. Drawings of red hearts surrounded them.
The pink bear had a ribbon in its hair, and someone had drawn a
train conductor's hat on the brown bear. Underneath the bears,
in the same ink, someone had written "Mikey & Margie." Inside
the card, in the same elegant handwriting—

Dear Sam,
     Please join Michael, Amanda and me for the celebration
of our thirty-second wedding anniversary, this coming
Thursday, May 29, at Whirly's. BIG secret: Mikey doesn't
know I had our super-8 movies converted to DVD, so
there will be a mandatory viewing of our wedding video
at our house after dinner—1976 fashions and all! (Wear

your bell-bottoms if you got 'em!) It will just be the three
of us unless you attend, so please bring a date if you like—
Mikey tells me you might have some news for us!
	Warmest regards,
	Margie Shield

Sam had burned the date into his brain: May 29 was the
night of the Chestnut Falls Village Council meeting.

In another life, Sam would have been happy to go to the
Shields' anniversary party: if Sophie were here; if something
had brought the two of them to this town of shot-up cops and
quarreling lovers and lifelong residents who seemed to give gifts
and offer help as a matter of daily life.

Yet in this life, this was the town of Lee Clayborne, and
Sophie was buried in Paris.

The party had one saving grace: Michael Shield would be
home and couldn't stand between him and Lee Clayborne. He
must have gotten a replacement for the council meeting.

Without Mike watching the meeting, Sam knew he could
do it now. He'd fire the gun until it was empty of its six bullets.
He'd take Clayborne by surprise until whoever took Sergeant
Shield's place that night had to draw and shoot him.

Sam felt his finger on the trigger and imagined bullets ripping
into Clayborne, whose own flesh and blood and heartbeat were
as fragile as anyone else's.

Before he'd come to this village, Sam had never thought of
shooting a human being, of shooting anything. Now he could
see no other way. He was here to confront evil, in the form of
Lee Clayborne.

Sam lunged from the kitchen chair, up the stairs, and into
the bathroom, where he vomited.

I'll be a killer, he thought. *As bad as him.*

When he had the strength, he stood up and washed his face and brushed his teeth. He walked back downstairs into the kitchen.

Sam wrapped the .38 Police Special back in the cheesecloth and put it in an empty drawer in the kitchen. He walked upstairs to his bedroom and pulled his bedclothes off the bed. He put a sheet on the floor, near the front door, but out of sight of anyone who would be standing at the window, and put a pillow down. He lay down and pulled a blanket over himself and closed his eyes.

Moments later, he got up. He took the box of bullets out of the paper bag that was still in the front hall, went back to the kitchen, and got the gun. He pushed the ejector pin and opened the barrel. Slowly, his hands steady, Sam loaded six bullets, then spun the cartridge and shut it, as he had seen Chet do. He wrapped the gun in the cheesecloth and put it back in the drawer. Then he took it back out, unwrapped it, and placed it on the floor next to where he was again going to lie down.

Before he lay on the floor, for the first time since he'd moved from his and Sophie's flat in Paris, Sam locked the door to his home.

Chapter Forty-Six

SAM STUCK THE GUN, empty again of bullets, in the back of his pants. Though the temperature was in the upper sixties, he wore his blue sweater over a shirt to hide the gun. He left the house through the front door and headed down to his office. He was determined to work until the end. Today he planned to write about Pomerol wines of Bordeaux, put the article in an envelope, walk to the post office, and send it to his editor.

Walking down Grove Hill, Sam saw Ellen and Adva walking toward him.

"Hey, you," Ellen said.

She put her arms around him and hugged him as he stood stiffly.

"Give me some sugar, Sugar," she said. "Didn't you get our thank-you note and key chain from Chicago? We thought you needed something to remind you of your hometown."

She pulled back and put her hands around his upper arms.

"Damn, you're uptight. I said a hug."

She hugged him harder and he hugged her back. The gun stuck out through his sweater in the back. Neither woman could see it.

"We missed you," Adva said, avoiding his eyes. "Thanks for taking care of Ringo."

"We were just talking about you," Ellen said. "Were your ears burning?"

"Not particularly," Sam said.

He smiled, pointed to the sky. "*Il fait beau aujourd'hui, Mesdames.*"

"Do you know what he said?" Ellen said.

"Something about nice weather," Adva said. "And he called us madams. Sounds sketchy."

"I think it sounds lovely. Everything okay?" Ellen said. "Spring is here. You have to be happy about that. And we're back. "

"Everything's great," Sam said. "It's good to see you. The town hasn't been the same since you left. And thanks for the gift."

"Do you have it? Are you using it?" Adva said. "Let's see." She smiled, wanting to get back to normal with Sam, who knew, and Ellen, who didn't. Maybe. She'd been looking at Adva differently lately.

"Haven't put my keys on it yet," Sam said. "I will today."

"Boys," Adva said.

The women took each other's hands and began moving past Sam when they paused to spin around. He turned just as they did so he faced them.

"Will you go to Blossom Time with us tomorrow night?" Ellen said. "Get tummy aches eating nasty food, ride the broken-down rides, yell at the carnies . . . partake of cherished Chestnut Falls traditions?"

"Tomorrow?"

"Opening night. Thursday. Biggest night of the year in Chestnut Falls. More people come back to town than at Christmastime," Adva said. "You either get into it, suffer through Beatles tribute bands, carnies on loudspeakers shouting at the kids, and lots and lots of motorcycles, drunks, and sirens, or you can suffer in your lonely house. Come on. It'll be fun."

"What time?" Sam said.

Adva and Ellen looked at each other.

"Seven?" Ellen said. "We'll go for an hour. We can get a drink afterward."

The Village Council meeting was to be over at about seven-thirty.

"I could meet you at eight, eight-thirty."

Adva walked toward Sam.

"That's too late; it closes at eight. What in the world do you have to do?"

Adva looked at Ellen, who was just behind her.

"Honey?"

Ellen fought her jealousy. She knew she had to trust; she had no option. Adva had hinted that Sam had some problem that he couldn't discuss and they'd left it at that.

"I'll see you at home."

Ellen turned and walked up Grove Hill.

"See you tomorrow night, Ellen," Sam said too loudly.

"Uh-huh," Ellen said, without turning around.

Adva looked in Sam's eyes. His back was facing town. He knew she still hadn't seen the handgun in his back pants.

"Warm day for a sweater, Sam."

"Not that warm, Adva. It gets chilly in the office. No sun until the late afternoon. All that brick upstairs cools things."

Adva sighed and tightened her lips. She'd cut her hair since they'd made love in his office. Her bangs hung over her thick dark eyebrows. She looked younger and less professionally severe. He wanted to touch her face and beg her forgiveness for what he was planning to do.

"I don't know where to begin," she said. "I'm sure you don't have a permit to carry. But that's the least of my worries."

She put her arms around him and patted the gun.

Sam remained silent.

"Where'd you get it?"

"Does it matter?"

"Did it occur to you that you could shoot yourself in the ass, Sam?"

Adva had tears in her eyes.

"I'm beyond upset. Don't let my crying fool you. I'm furious. What are you thinking?"

"It's not loaded. It's for protection."

Adva shook her head. She looked around. Police were walking the streets, casually, chatting with townies and tourists. She worked with enough of them through the schools to know that half were gung-ho young ones, barely out of the academy, and half were part-bored part-timers who had retired from forces in New York and Cleveland. They all could spot a badly concealed handgun from a hundred paces.

"I'm going to walk with you to your office. Right behind you. I'll act like I'm teasing you, too close, maybe a little drunk and obnoxious. Okay? Don't walk too fast. Now move. Move!"

He trusted Adva: he obeyed. They walked a half a block. Adva waved at two cops she knew. To one of the older ones across the street, one who began to look at Sam, she called out, "Hey, Mayford . . . you like my new haircut?" She shook it, not her style to do so, but Mayford grinned.

"Looking good, Doc," he called out. "Yeah, I like the new hairdo!"

He turned to talk to a family of tourists.

"Hurry," Adva said.

The door was locked.

"Keys, Sam?"

Sam tried the door. "I don't understand. This door is usually open at this time of day," he said. "I keep the key to my office over the door upstairs." He went through his pockets. No keys.

"Don't look to your right," Adva said, her voice strained and urgent. "Keep looking for your keys."

Sam looked to his right. Stomping straight at them, dressed in jeans and a black T-shirt that was just tight enough to show off his well-muscled body, wearing black loafers and no socks, laughing with one of his buddies, was Lee Clayborne.

He'd seen Adva and Sam from a half block away, just past the bridge over the river, which was swollen from the rains the day before. His friend was chattering. Lee stopped smiling and put his hand up in front of his friend's face.

"Shut up," he said to his friend.

"Sam, turn around," Adva said.

Sam did. Adva grabbed the back of his head. She pushed him into the doorway to his office, nearly breaking the glass on the door. She kissed him. He resisted enough so that she put her mouth to his ear and said, "Kiss me as if your life depended on it. Kiss me like you did before."

As Lee Clayborne moved closer to Sam and Adva, the couple began to kiss, mouths moving, tongues just touching, like lovers.

Lee was next to them. His face was on fire, upper lip curled.

Adva turned from Sam to Lee. "Oh, it's *you*. This is none of your business. Keep moving or"—she nodded toward Mayford, the police officer in the crosswalk—"I'll tell the cops you just violated your restraining order. It'll tie you up for tonight. I know how important it is to you to check out the new *talent* in town. Asshole."

Adva looked up at Lee and stared him straight in the eyes.

"If you want to hit somebody, hit me, tough guy. But do it in public," she said.

Lee was silent.

"Coward," Adva said.

Lee looked from Adva to Sam. He clenched his fists; his feet were in a pose to hit hard.

"I know why you're here, you phony frog punk. I was only wrong about who you're after," Lee said to Sam. "So you're doing my ex-wife. Either way, you're a snake. I was right about that."

He looked at Adva and smirked. Sam thought he'd never seen a smirk that looked so violent, as if it alone could kill.

Lee crossed his arms and glowered at Sam. "Get lonely over there in France, punk? Dead wife and all? You couldn't get some Paris pussy?"

Sam, blind now with hatred, moved at Lee. Mayford's head whipped around, watching a potential fight unfold.

"Sam, no! Please!" Adva said, then whispered, her voice breaking, "Enough, Sam. This needs to end."

Lee, through with Sam for now, looked back at Adva. "But of course: *her*. This is too perfect, dude!" He nodded at Adva and laughed.

"And you," he yelled to Adva. "Talk about predictable. Does your dyke know you threw her over for a piece of Euro-trash?" he said.

"Don't test me," Adva said, but her voice was now shaking. "You know that's a bad idea."

His friend following him, Lee acted as if he were ignoring Adva's comment and began a diagonal jaywalk move across Main, in full view of the cop at the crosswalk. He stopped in the middle of the street and looked back at Sam.

"She may be a lesbian," he called out. "But she'll ride you like . . ."

He pointed to the Ferris wheel and both Lee and his friend burst out laughing.

"Couldn't happen to a nicer guy," Lee said louder. "Keep up the good work with your women, Pierre."

Lee stood in the middle of the street, defying Mayford, and the cars that swerved to avoid him. "I know who you are, Koppang. Maybe you like my sloppy seconds, huh? Just stay away from Rachel. That," Lee said, making his right hand into a gun, "would really piss me off." He made a clicking sound, and then, "Bang, Sammy."

Lee looked at Adva, smiled, then looked back at Sam.

"I'll be seeing you around, Koppang," Lee shouted. "Count on it."

Sam knew it was time to tell Ellen what Adva already knew. Over coffee at their house, Adva and Ellen listened as Sam slalomed his way through lies and facts. The facts—his hatred for Lee, his decision to look his wife's killer in the face, even knowing who he was—had all been true.

He told them about buying the gun at the store in Pennsylvania. He assured them that he realized it was a bad idea, and that he would take it back.

As he prepared to leave Adva and Ellen's home, Sam hugged them both.

"One last thing," Ellen said. "Is she or is she not a good kisser?"

Sam's face blushed uncontrollably.

"Yes, she is." He looked at Adva. "Yes, you are."

"So are you, Sam," she said. "You shouldn't waste that. You have love left. There will be passion, if you let it happen. Life does go on."

Ellen and Sam saw she was crying. Adva went back in the house.

"Sam?" Ellen said. "I said I'd love you as a friend if you told the truth. But I know about what happened with you and Adva. I'm so hurt, Sam. I'm so hurt. And I don't know if I can ever forgive you. I will eventually, I suppose. Because I saw it coming, probably before you did. Before she did. Adva and I are in love, Sam. I don't know what else to say."

Stunned, Sam climbed the hill to his house. He looked back at Adva and Ellen's deck. Adva walked back outside. Ellen turned around, and they held each other, their eyes closed.

That night, his loaded gun next to him in his makeshift bed by the front hallway, Sam thought of Adva and Ellen, of Micheline and Erasmo, of Mom and Pop, of Michael and Margie, and of his life with Sophie. Finally, at a little after 5:00 a.m., he fell asleep and slept without dreaming.

On Thursday, with a clear head and a calm, cold heart, Sam Koppang awoke a little after noon. He made coffee in the coffeemaker Ellen had given him. He ate the last of some bread and cheese he'd gotten at the local supermarket. He showered, shaved, and dressed. This time he put the loaded .38 into his small suitcase and left the house without locking the door.

When he arrived at his office, he sat down at his desk to wait through the day. Just after two-thirty, families began to populate the village, especially near his office. On the other side of the southern-facing brick wall, Blossom Time had begun.

Downtown was exuberant: children jumped up and down, skipped, ran, sauntered, walked with all the time in the world, the holiday weekend joyously before them and the end of school not far off. The younger ones strained against parents, the older ones roamed in small, emancipated groups, harmless to all but their own imaginations.

Music from the carnival rides began: old heavy rock and roll, AC/DC, Led Zeppelin, Aerosmith. Jaycees made announcements about hot-air balloon races scheduled for after dark that evening, up Washington Street, behind the Chestnut Falls High School campus.

Through his open window Sam smelled sausages with onions and peppers, hot dogs, popcorn, deep-fried elephant ears, steamed pretzels with mustard, cotton candy—all mixed with the rural smell of the straw that had been spread over the grass of Riverside Park. The carnival setup crew had ripped up the grass; the rains from two days before had turned the dirt to mud. Now the straw remained dry under the clear skies and dried mud.

The sun arched from Sam's left to right and began its descent over the Town Hall. Sam watched the town go about its business and its pleasure, and waited for evening.

Chapter Forty-Seven

LEE CLAYBORNE OWNED NINE suits. This evening he picked the dark blue Belvest. He matched the wool suit that felt like silk with a white Kiton cotton shirt that felt like satin, a tangerine Hermès tie decorated with white abstract horses, and black John Lobb lace-up shoes. He calculated that his outfit cost about six thousand dollars.

The wall safe in his library receded into the stucco wall painted deep green, behind a hunting painting he'd bought in Scotland for three thousand dollars. Lee liked the classic sensibility of a wall safe behind a painting. He liked classic things: the best things, things that last.

Dressed and shaved, teeth brushed, blond hair falling boyishly over his forehead, Lee channeled his disgust at Adva and Koppang's public display—what a sick hookup, what a perfect duo, the lesbian and the loser—into the frustration that had built up in him, day after day, night after night, even in his dreams, over his plummeting business, over Rachel Rosen, over everything.

His hatred for Johnny Kenston grew alongside his passion for Rachel like morning-glory vines: entwined, indistinguishable from each other, becoming one. He wanted him dead. Kenston had come between him and Rachel. Then he'd find Koppang. If he wasn't at Whirly's, Lee knew where he lived.

Lee looked down at his manicured fingernails as he turned

the safe's dial. The combination was 10-7-42, his mother's birthday. He reached his hand into his safe and took out a silver 9mm Heckler & Koch handgun in its custom-made brown leather holster that a grateful lumber supplier, an amateur leathersmith, had made for Lee. The leathersmith had engraved his initials, *LC*, in the middle of the hand-tooled mountain range.

Now and then Lee would take the semiautomatic H&K out to oil it and check the magazine.

"I want the best handgun available" were the only words he'd said to the dealer not five miles from his home, where he bought the firearm legally and went patiently through the waiting period six years earlier.

Afterward, he'd put the gun in the safe, where he'd kept it since he renovated the house after his divorce from Adva. Tonight he took it out and put it in his messenger bag, along with a legal pad and the Churchill book and another on architecture. He placed the gun in the holster in the middle of the bag, shook it to make sure it wasn't discernible. He slung the bag over his shoulder and walked out of the house, locked the door behind him, and walked to the Town Hall, where he'd preside over the council meeting.

Chapter Forty-Eight

Lee walked up the steps to the Town Hall and past the council people who waited on the steps until the last minute, breathing in the spring air.

Inside, Lee was startled to see the police chief and briefly wondered where Sergeant Shield was.

"Chief," Clayborne said, nodding and smiling at Chief of Police Steve Getzer. "Good to see you working." The two men laughed together.

Sitting at the middle of the large table, Council President Lee Clayborne called the meeting to order. The minutes of the last meeting passed.

Lee Clayborne, as part of a long-standing tradition in the village, declared that all village business could wait because Blossom Time started tonight.

"Let's be with our families and friends tonight and enjoy the festival," he said. "Get outside and watch the hot-air balloons. I'll see you there."

And then he uttered the traditional declaration by the council president on the first night of Blossom Time: "Politics can wait."

Chapter Forty-Nine

THOUGH SAM WAS STARTLED at how quickly the meeting ended and Clayborne exited the Town Hall, the moment he saw him from his window Sam moved in concert with him. He grabbed the loaded .38, stuck it into the back of his pants, underneath his blue sweater, left his office, moved fast down the narrow stairs, left hand on the railing, right hand sliding on the plaster wall, bracing himself. He had come too far, suffered too much to fail now.

Sam opened the door onto Main Street. To his right, a mother and father pushing a stroller with twins walked toward him. He would have to shoot Lee point blank, away from any bystanders. Mayford the cop was in the crosswalk to his left and waved to the chief, who was headed to his car and back home. Sam stepped off the sidewalk and into the street.

Lee was walking down Main Street toward J's, where Sam knew he met friends after his council meetings. By the middle of the street, Sam saw that Clayborne was dressed up. He looked out of place on this casual small-town evening. Clayborne looked like an elegant Parisian businessman hurrying down the Champs-Élysées to an appointment.

But Clayborne passed J's without looking inside. Where's he going? Sam wondered. He moved quickly and Sam kept pace with him. Sam moved his hand so he could easily reach his gun. Past J's, Lee picked up his pace.

Sam stayed about ten feet behind, far enough to grab for his gun before Clayborne could get to him should he turn around. He must be heading up Grove Hill toward Sam's. That was the only place he could go at the north end of town.

Except for Whirly's.

Chapter Fifty

THE SIDEWALK WAS BLOCKED by the time Sam reached a boutique near Whirly's. Straining his neck, he couldn't see Clayborne. The crowd was three rows deep: middle-aged bikers, a family of five, a pack of teenagers. Sam couldn't risk pushing people out of the way and drawing attention to himself. He wove threw them slowly.

"Excuse me," he kept repeating until he bumped hard into one of the leather-clad bikers.

"Easy, bro, easy," an old biker said, turning around as Sam tried to push past him. "Chill out. It's Blossom Time."

Sam was startled. The biker's face was a road map of experience and rough times. It reminded Sam of Mike Shields's face, though capped by a bandanna instead of a police hat. The biker looked into Sam's eyes.

"What's going on, bro?" he said. He moved to block Sam's path, held him on by the shoulders. "You okay?"

Sam stared at him. "You've got to let me go."

Time stopped for Sam. "Please. I don't want to fight you. Just let me move on."

The biker studied Sam's eyes.

"Go," the biker said.

*   *   *

Clayborne was moving away. He was now slowly weaving his way through the crowd, too. Sam hadn't lost him.

Sam ran toward him. He reached back for his gun and touched it, grabbed it and began to bring it forward.

Then, five feet behind Lee Clayborne, Sam stopped, suddenly, in the middle of the sidewalk. He tasted something. At first he thought it was blood. And then he knew: it was wine.

Erasmo's brother's wine. Just as quickly, it disappeared from his mouth and moved into his blood and right through his body. *To replace your poisoned blood so you can live,* Erasmo had said.

Sam stood still. He took his hand off of the gun. He heard the rush of the nearby waterfall in his ears.

"There's nothing I could have done, Sophie," he said aloud. "I couldn't save you."

On the sidewalk of a village in the midwestern United States, Sam Koppang knew it was over. The poison had simply drained out of him and was gone.

Sam quickly put the gun in the back of his pants and out of sight. He looked around. In the near frenzy of Blossom Time, no one had noticed.

He stood and watched Lee Clayborne move down the street. He saw a man on his way to the rest of his life, whatever that wretched life might hold. Wherever he was going, Sam no longer wished to follow.

He watched Clayborne disappear inside Whirly's. Then Sam turned around and walked across the street and up the stairs, into his office. He emptied his gun of bullets. He wrapped it in the red cheesecloth. He sat down at his typewriter and realized it was time to say good-bye.

And then he remembered Clayborne's words in the street days earlier: "Bang, Sammy."

Chapter Fifty-One

RACHEL ROSEN UNCORKED A bottle of Moët et Chandon White Star Champagne. The table in the corner near the window erupted in cheers. She slowly poured a glass and smiled.

"I have to do this slowly, you guys," she shouted to the crowd of mostly twenty- and thirty-somethings who had come home from Chicago, Boston, San Francisco, and elsewhere for Blossom Time. "For a special occasion like this."

As she poured the second glass, the front door of Whirly's opened. For a moment, she didn't recognize the handsome, well-dressed man with the messenger bag who walked through and smiled at her from halfway between the door and the bar.

"Hey, Rachel. You look gorgeous as ever," said a smiling Lee Clayborne.

Rachel Rosen didn't move. She called out, "Johnny." Then louder: "Johnny. Johnny!"

Johnny Kenston came out of the back kitchen. He wiped his hands on his apron without taking his eyes off a still smiling Clayborne, who looked at him as he unzipped his messenger bag.

"Clayborne," Johnny said evenly. "You're not welcome here. You know that. You have to leave."

Lee's mouth twisted and he cocked his head. "Um . . . no. No. Wrong answer, Johnny. Completely wrong answer."

Lee stopped unzipping the bag and put his hands up.

"See, it's you who aren't welcome. Not because you're black, Johnny. Not because you're a psycho Vietnam vet, Johnny. That's not why you're not welcome in this town."

"Johnny?" Rachel said. "Should I call the police?"

"Bad idea, Rachel," Lee said.

He finished unzipping the messenger bag. He let his empty hands fall.

"We're all good, Rachel," Lee said. "I'm just stopping by to say hi before I go and visit my buddy Sam up the hill. You know Sam, right? I need to give him something."

"That's okay, Rachel," Johnny said, staring at the messenger bag. "It's cool."

Lee looked at Rachel and took a step forward.

Johnny Kenston had seen this expression before, in Vietnam. Something had gone very wrong in Clayborne.

"Are you cool, Lee?" Johnny said.

"Actually, I'm not cool. I'm not finished."

He stared hard at Johnny.

"You're not welcome here anymore because you don't get me. Because you fucked up my life and now *she* doesn't get me. You kept me from her. You embarrassed me. You and Koppang. You're in it together."

Lee withdrew the H&K from the messenger bag and, in rapid movements, pointed it at Johnny, then at Rachel, then back at Johnny.

Outside, Sam passed a store selling Oriental rugs and reached Whirly's a few seconds after Lee Clayborne. He opened the door and ran inside.

Still moving forward, Sam Koppang of the South Side of Chicago, and Paris, and Ville de Rachat, took a split second to realize what he saw in front of him: a gun in Lee Clayborne's shaking hand, pointed alternately at Johnny and then at Rachel.

Sam dove four feet toward Clayborne. He wrapped his hands around his waist and brought him down in a perfect tackle. As Clayborne fell, he fired, sending a bullet into a bottle of Absolut Vodka, shattering two other bottles on the shelf behind the bar with its shards.

He held onto his gun, and jumped to his feet before Sam, who breathed heavily, could move. Sam stood and shifted toward Clayborne. Lee raised his gun and pointed it again at Johnny.

"Stop! These people have done nothing to you. I'm the one after you. Not them. You killed my wife. Sophie."

Lee cocked his head and laughed. "Sophie was your wife? No shit? I didn't kill her." He burst out laughing. "But that's too good. We have a lot in common, Sammy. A lot in common." Lee smiled and moved his gun, pointing it at Sam's face. "There really can't be two of us, can there? This is my town, Sammy." He shoved the gun barrel onto Sam's forehead.

A young woman sitting to Sam and Lee's left screamed, and Lee turned his head to see what was happening.

Three rounds fired from a Glock 17 9mm semiautomatic entered the right side of Lee Clayborne's chest within inches of one another. Clayborne was dead before he hit the ground. His gun went off a second time as he fell, a single bullet shattering a window and lodging in the side of a Cadillac Escalade's front end parked in front of Whirly's.

Some of the Whirly's patrons had dropped to the floor, squatting or lying face down, thinking more gunfire would follow. Some of them remained standing and joined the young woman and screamed; some stood and said nothing.

In the corner by the window, with smoke coming out of the barrel of his police-issued pistol, standing in a white disco suit and wide-collared black shirt, both of which no longer fit—his

face blank, his wife screaming, his daughter crying—was retired
New York City Street Crimes Detective, Chestnut Falls Police
Sergeant Michael Shield.

Chapter Fifty-Two

WHIRLY'S MAIN STREET GRILL—Johnny Kenston's pride and joy and redemption after the violence of Vietnam—was cordoned off as a crime scene.

Glass shards from the bottles and window covered the floor. Some people cried. Some held their faces in their hands.

As six officers began clearing the room, taking witnesses outside to be interviewed, Sam walked toward Michael Shield, then stopped.

He looked at Lee's face one last time. Lee stared out at his eternity. Wherever he was now was lost to Sam.

Four Chestnut Falls paramedics, who had arrived at the same time as the police, bent down, checked Lee, covered his face and body with a blanket.

Rachel, Amanda, and Margie huddled at a table. Rachel trembled uncontrollably. Margie and Amanda put their arms around her, wrapping her until she disappeared under their protection.

Michael Shield and Johnny Kenston sat down a table near the fireplace and talked to Chief Getzer, who had been on his way home from the Village Council meeting when dispatch radioed him that there had been a shooting at Whirly's.

Sam walked over to their table. He looked down at Michael Shield, who looked up at Sam. Michael smiled weakly. They both ignored the covered body of Lee Clayborne that lay so close to them.

"We didn't think you were coming," Shield said. "But I'm glad you made it."

Michael Shield and Sam Koppang looked over at Margie, dressed in a silver-sparkle wraparound dress, and Amanda, in her big denim bell-bottoms, peasant top, headband, and platform shoes. They couldn't even see Rachel huddled among the two women's 1970s outfits.

"Some party, huh?" Shield said. "I'll talk to you later, okay, Sam? I'll have some time to smoke one of those Cubans with you. I'll be on administrative leave for a while."

He held his big hand out to Sam, who took it in both of his.

"You saved Rachel, Sam. Or Johnny. Or both," Michael said.

"You saved my life, Mike," Sam said. "I don't know what to say. Thank you doesn't seem like enough."

"Oh, no. We're even," said Michael.

"How?" Sam asked.

"I needed backup. You were there. He could've shot the place up. Margie, Mandy, too," Shield said.

The two men stood for a few moments.

"There's only one hero here, Mike," Sam said. "I'm looking at him."

"Let's talk later, okay?" Michael replied, quickly wiping his eyes. "I'm going to be pretty busy here."

"Do you need me to make a statement or anything?" Sam said.

"We've got plenty of witnesses, Sam. For now, go home and get some rest. We'll be in touch if we need to talk to you. From what I saw—what everyone saw, you walked into a bar and tackled a man about to commit at least one murder. I imagine the TV folks will want to interview you."

"But, Mike. I need to tell you—" Sam said.

"You walked in here and tackled a man pointing a gun at two people," Michael said, this time with force in his voice. "That's exactly what happened. Everyone saw it. You were a defensive back in high school, right? Seems like you should've been first string."

"Hell of a memory, Mike," Sam said.

There was a pause as Michael looked at Sam. It seemed like a long time since their meeting at the top of Grove Hill, when he'd instantly liked this stranger but wondered about him, worried about him and why he was there. So much had changed, but now he knew what kind of man Sam was.

"I think you've had enough trouble," Michael said. "Haven't you, Sam? Now go home, my friend."

The two men hugged. Sam's eyes clouded with tears and he didn't want to look Michael Shield in the eye. Michael Shield avoided Sam's for the same reason. Finally they pulled back.

"I have to leave, Mike."

"I heard what was said here, Sam. I figured as much. I'll miss you. Margie will too." He looked over at Rachel and Johnny, who were talking to the detective. "Them too. All of us will. What about your friends up the hill, Sam? Are you sure? They really care about you."

Sam couldn't speak.

"Just know you have a home here, Sam. Anytime. Marge and Mandy and I found our home. Maybe you could, too. Sometimes home isn't where the heart is. It's where other people's hearts are, the people who care about you. Sometimes that's how you find yours."

"There are some things I need to do back in France."

"Of course. And Sam? We have an old expression here. Surely

you remember it: You're one of the good guys. Do *you* know that?"

Sam didn't answer. He and Michael Shield shook hands. Michael turned back to his family and hugged Amanda and Margie. As Sam reached the door to leave, he turned around. Johnny was looking at him. He gave Sam an informal salute and a nod. Sam did the same back to Johnny Kenston, the Vietnam veteran who would, he thought, finally have a chance to enjoy his retirement and get some rest.

Sam left Whirly's Main Street Grill for his house up the hill.

Chapter Fifty-Three

THAT NIGHT SAM DROVE to Chet's store in Pennsylvania. It was closed, so he placed a taped-up, corrugated box on which he had written, "Chet/Personal," in front of the store, but to the right of the cement steps, out of sight of anyone driving by. Inside the box the gun was wrapped in the red cheesecloth. An enclosed note read:

> I changed my mind about the gun. I guess I'll take my chances. Here it is, along with all the bullets. I owe you for the food and coffee. This should cover it. I wish you well.

When he arrived home, Sam wrote another note, this one to Jimmy Schultz.

> Jimmy,
> Things have changed for me, and I've had to leave unexpectedly. I've signed the truck title back to you and enclosed the rent for the rest of my lease.
> I have one favor: The cash I've enclosed should also cover the shipping of the typewriter to the enclosed address. I've gotten used to it. Thanks again for it and for everything else. I'll miss this place.
> —Sam

Sam wrote out his address at Ville de Rachat. At two o'clock in the morning, Sam put the truck keys, his office keys, and the envelope with the note and address through the mail slot of the Chestnut Valley Hardware Store.

He walked back to his house and put the key on the hall table, where he'd found it five months earlier. On the same table he left a gift-wrapped box of Cuban cigars with a note to his Realtor to give the gift to Sergeant Michael Shield of the Chestnut Falls Police Department—at his home. Sam took his small suitcase and put the black gloves that Ellen and Adva had given him and put them on top of clothes. He sat on the steps outside the rental house as he waited for the taxi to the airport that he'd called from the last remaining phone booth in Chestnut Falls.

"Stop on the first corner, please," Sam said to the cab driver. "Right here."

He got out of the car and walked up to Ellen and Adva's front porch. They, like most of the townspeople, were still asleep. He placed two bottles of 1998 Veuve Clicquot La Grande Dame Champagne that he'd bought at Kurt's Fine Wines in the village, and placed a note in the ribbon on top of one of the gift boxes.

> Dear Adva and Ellen,
> I've left for France. I got this for a special occasion for you two. Somehow I never got around to giving it. No need to wait for the new year—it should be perfect to drink right now. Sip it slowly or guzzle it quickly, but drink it together.
> Part of me will always be here.
> I love you both,
> —Sam

As the taxi drove Sam through town on the way to the freeway and airport, he asked the driver to slow down and stop for a moment at the Village Triangle. Sam opened the window of the taxi and breathed in the late May air. He smiled at the smell of the apple blossoms lining the Triangle. It was sweet and fresh inside The Bubble, as if someone had cracked it open.

"Okay," Sam said to the cab driver. "To the airport. I'm ready to go home."

Epilogue

THE HUGE TREE AT le parc Monceau seemed unchanged. Sam put his arms around it as far as he could.

"I love you, Sophie. Can you feel it?" he whispered.

Sam held the tree for several minutes. His tears darkened the bark just as the bark etched his face with its antiquity.

Then he turned and left the le parc Monceau, and Paris.

Truffaut sat on the front porch of the cottage in Ville de Rachat, as if he had been expecting Sam. Sam leaned down and picked up him up and stroked his chin. The yellow cat purred and licked Sam's earlobe. After a minute, he squirmed and Sam put him back on the stone walkway. Truffaut trotted away to stretch out and rest in the lavender, out of the sun.

At either side of the doorway there were baskets of flowers. Sam recognized them from Micheline's garden. He opened the unlocked door and saw that again Micheline and Erasmo had laden the table with bread, cheese, and fruit from the market.

In the center of the table was a bottle of wine with no label. Sam heard steps. They stopped. Erasmo stood in the doorway.

"*Entrez dans ma maison, s'il vous plaît, mon ami*," Sam said.

"Let me look at your face, Sam."

Erasmo entered as Sam had asked him to do. He walked to Sam and took his face in his hands.

"Let us sit."

"It's good to see you, Erasmo."

"The eyes in this face . . ." He again took Sam's face in his hands. "And the face itself. It is changed."

"How are you, Erasmo?"

"Micheline and I are well. We argue and we make love." He smiled. "Our life is of one passion or another, but always the passion is there."

"I'm happy to hear that."

Erasmo picked up the bottle of wine.

"The wine of my brother. Do you remember?"

"Yes, of course."

"*L'âme du vin*. The soul of wine. Do you remember this, too?"

"I do."

Erasmo took a corkscrew out of his pocket. He opened the bottle.

"One moment to breathe," he said.

Sam began to stand, but Erasmo put his large hand on Sam's arm.

"You sit now."

Erasmo walked to the sink, took two dusty wineglasses, turned on the faucet, let the rust run through the pipes. He rinsed the glasses. He took a kerchief out of his pocket and dried them.

"Clean," he said.

Erasmo poured two glasses of wine and placed them on the table. A soft sea breeze came in through the window.

They sat and let the wine breathe a while longer in the glasses. Sam inhaled. He had missed the salt air.

"Did you do what you needed to do, Sam?"

"Yes."

"Your face tells me you can finally taste this wine."

The two men drank the wine of Erasmo's brother, the wine into which he had put his soul.

"I want to ask you another question, Sam."

"Of course."

"In all the time you lived here before, we never heard you sing. Even when we sang, you would stay silent."

"I used to sing to Sophie."

"Would you like me to teach you to sing again?"

"Very much."

And so, through the night, Erasmo taught Sam French folksongs that his family had sung for generations. The two men talked and sang until the sun rose behind the cottage.

In the forgiving light of dawn, Erasmo left to join his sleeping wife next door. Sam lay down on the bed in his home, his heart quiet, alone in his soul at last, and slept.

Acknowledgments

I wrote *Vengeance Follows* over a period of twelve years. It began one evening when I went alone to a French café in Greenwich Village, not long after 9/11. I spent four hours observing the café and taking notes, reading the Sunday *Times*, slowly eating my dinner, and working on a bottle of French Buzet wine. New York City was where I wrote the first and last line of *The Year That Trembled*, my first novel, and the city was where the idea of this novel hatched on that night in a city that had been stunned by tragedy.

Along the way, a number of people helped me in various ways, such as Abigail Montague, Nellie Bridge and Hector Lugo, the intrepid Web Services team at the Authors Guild. I am grateful to Curtis Taylor for sharing his knowledge of firearms; to Janet Loftus, Certified Specialist of Wine; Chief James Brosius and Detective Tim Reed of the Chagrin Falls Police Department; Madame Fadia Hamid, teacher of French and Arabic at my alma mater, Chagrin Falls High School; the folks from Chagrin Hardware & Supply—Susie Johnson Shutts, Ken Jr., Jack and Steve Shutts, and Rob Schwind; Larry Shibley, Henry "Woody" Needham, and Michael Collins. My special thanks go to my manager and friend, Jim McSherry.

While New York was where my first two novels took wing, the Cleveland area, and in particular Chagrin Falls, is where I find much of the inspiration for my fiction. It seems fitting, then, that Cleveland is where I met a publisher and the people in his company who gave a second life to my first novel, as well as life to this one. Their tireless effort to the art of literature is profound. And so I thank my incisive and excellent editor, Jennifer Sawyer Fisher, my expert copyeditor Rosalie Wieder, and the Gray & Co. team that worked on this book with me: the creative Jane Lassar, the rock-steady Chris Andrikanich, the eagle-eyed Rob Lucas, and the visionary David Gray.

When I began this novel all of the other members of my birth family were alive. So to my courageous sister Pat, my loving Norwegian-American mother Jo, and my dad Mel—who, in the words of James Taylor, was "soft as smoke and tough as nails"—I thank them in memoriam.

To my stepson Angus and my son Finn Scott, I give heartfelt thanks for making my work of storytelling that much more meaningful to me.

Last and certainly not least, it was not until I met my wife, Lydia—more than five years after that solemn evening in New York City, when I decided to set a love story in a French café—that I found the heart of this novel, It was Lydia who urged me on to keep writing, through trying times, and it is to she to whom I offer my deepest loving gratitude.

About the Author

SCOTT LAX IS A novelist, short story writer, playwright, film and television writer, and writing teacher. As a columnist and essayist he's had hundreds of essays published about a diverse range of topics ranging from politics to culture to fatherhood to wine. He has also worked as a salesman and a professional musician (performing as a drummer with Bo Diddley, among others). He studied Shakespeare at the University of Cambridge while studying at Hiram College, from which he graduated with a degree in English. Scott Lax was a Bread Loaf Scholar in nonfiction and a Sewanee Fellow in fiction. He was named Midwest filmmaker of the year at the Cleveland International Film Festival in 2002 for his work as source-writer and producer of the film adaptation of his first novel, *The Year That Trembled.* Scott lives with his wife Lydia, son Finn Scott, and stepson, Angus, in the Chagrin Valley near Cleveland, Ohio.

For more information, event listings, short fiction, and news about Scott Lax's next book, visit:

www.ScottLax.com